"What are you doing here?"

"_____

K_____

y_____er
and doing her best to look stubborn, something
that had his mouth twitching, trying to hold back
a smile.

She was not a stubborn woman. She couldn't
be intimidating if she tried, and the only reason
he would ever be scared of her was in thinking
about his own temporary insanity, which he
blamed on her.

Which reminded him, he was trying to make up
for that.

Which meant, he had to make her listen to him
and come back home.

No time for Mr. Nice Guy, not that she'd ever
believe that of him again.

"Well, I have something to say to you," he said.
"And you're going to listen."

Dear Reader,

I love people with a plan, people who think they've figured out what's right and are trying to do it.

Joe Reed had a plan. He was going to marry Kate Cassidy. They were perfect for each other. Everyone thought so.

Then Kate's sister, Kathie, kissed Joe, and before shock or surprise took over, Joe kissed Kathie back. And liked it.

That's when his perfectly safe, predictable life plan fell apart.

I should probably mention, I love it, too, when people's nice, safe plans fall apart. It makes things so interesting.

Want to know who a man really is? Watch what happens when his life falls apart. That's when you find out what he's really made of.

Hope you enjoy it.

Teresa Hill

HER SISTER'S
FIANCÉ

TERESA HILL

SPECIAL EDITION®

Published by Silhouette Books

America's Publisher of Contemporary Romance

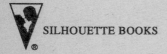 SILHOUETTE BOOKS

ISBN-13: 978-0-373-28041-4
ISBN-10:   0-373-28041-6

HER SISTER'S FIANCÉ

Copyright © 2006 by Teresa Hill

Printed in U.S.A.

Books by Teresa Hill (under the name Sally Tyler Hayes)

Silhouette Special Edition

Magic in a Jelly Jar #1390
*Heard It Through the Grapevine #1546
*A Little Bit Engaged #1740
*Her Sister's Fiancé #1743

Silhouette Intimate Moments

Whose Child is This? #439
Dixon's Bluff #485
Days Gone By #549
Not His Wife #611
Our Child? #671
Homecoming #700
Temporary Family #738
Second Father #753
Wife, Mother...Lover? #818
†Dangerous To Love #903
†Spies, Lies and Lovers #940
†Cinderella and the Spy #1001
†Her Secret Guardian #1012

*under the name Teresa Hill
†Division One

TERESA HILL

lives in South Carolina with her husband, son and daughter. A former journalist for a South Carolina newspaper, she fondly remembers that her decision to write and explore the frontiers of romance came at about the same time she discovered, in junior high, that she'd never be able to join the crew of the *Starship Enterprise*.

Happy and proud to be a stay-home mom, she is thrilled to be living her lifelong dream of writing romances.

To everyone at The Whole You, Rutherfordton, NC.
Without a doubt, some of the coolest, nicest,
funniest, kindest, most interesting people in the
world. (The only other group I've ever found that
I'd describe that way are romance writers.)
I love you all. We don't really have to leave, right?

And for Michael, because that's
just the way he is and because he asked,
I will write words I have never before used in
all of my twenty-three published novels:
Heaving Bosoms.
Heaving Bosoms.
Heaving Bosoms.

Chapter One

The little old ladies by the picnic tables glared at him like he was pond scum.

Joe Reed tried to ignore them as he stood under a giant magnolia tree eating a hot dog at the town's May Day picnic, trying to look like the old him—respectable, predictable, an all-around good guy.

Wait a minute. He leaned to the right to get a better look at one of the little old ladies.

Was that a friend of his grandmother's?

He groaned.

His grandmother was hard of hearing and not quite living in the present. She often thought she was a girl looking for her poodle, CoCo, who'd been dead for seventy-five years. Joe had hoped she'd never get the whole story of his downfall, but if one of her friends from the nursing home was here, she'd probably be treated to the whole unsavory thing. Which meant, he had to hope his grandmother either wouldn't hear what the woman had to say or that she'd forget it very quickly, both highly likely.

Still, he really didn't want her to know.

Yeah, now that he'd gotten a better look, he was afraid that was her friend Marge and…maybe she was coming this way, probably to give him a piece of her mind. He turned around hoping to disappear, but the next moment, he got nailed in the shoulders and dragged off into the woods by two men.

Not strangers, unfortunately.

He'd rather be mugged.

Not that anybody got mugged in Magnolia Falls, Georgia.

But he'd rather.

"Hey, come on," he tried.

Wherever they were going, he could at least get there under his own power. But his captors would have none of that, and one of them was armed, so he stopped arguing and let them do what they wanted.

They released him a half mile later, dumped him with his back against a tree, then backed up to face him, both glaring.

One was a cop.

Joe used to date his sister.

The other was a minister.

He was now married to the sister Joe used to date. Very happily married, by all accounts, so, as Joe saw it, Ben couldn't object too much to the fact that Joe and Kate had broken up. Otherwise, Ben and Kate would never have gotten together.

It was just the way in which Joe and Kate had broken up that was the problem.

That was where the other sister came into it. Kathie.

There was a third sister, Kim, the baby of the family, but Joe had never laid a hand on her.

It was the middle one who had been his downfall. Still was, judging by the way the people of their little town were treating him six months after the whole debacle.

"We have a problem," the brother who was the cop, Jax, said.

"Whatever it is, I didn't do it," Joe insisted, feeling like he was in third grade and had gotten caught pulling Celia Rawlins' hair. Not that he'd actually done it. She had just kept accusing him of it to get him into trouble. His mother said it was a crude form of flirtation, but he just hadn't understood. He didn't like being in trouble. He really was a good guy. Not that anybody believed that anymore.

"Oh, yes, you did," Jax said, looking as big and

intimidating as he had in high school, whether he'd been plowing through linebackers like they were zombies or dating the girls of the cheerleading squad one after another. Everybody got a turn. He'd made it look easy, still did.

Joe had been quieter, spent more time on his studies, been president of the senior class and valedictorian, a chess champion, a force to be reckoned with in debate, none of which had helped him get girls.

He was not a ladies' man, not at all the type to be engaged to one sister and sneaking around kissing the other.

He still wasn't sure how it had happened.

Temporary insanity was all he'd managed to come up with.

It still made his head spin when he thought about it too much, so he tried not to. He was a bank president, for God's sake. The youngest in the state when he'd been named to the job. Voted most likely to succeed. Mr. Straightlaced.

What had happened to that man?

"I really didn't do anything," Joe tried again.

He hadn't called anyone, hadn't talked to anyone, hadn't seen anyone. He'd lived the life of a monk for six months, trying to keep his head down and do his job and not give anyone reason to talk about him, not ever again.

Not that it had stopped any of the gossip.

He felt like he'd been branded for life, would never live down what had happened.

He looked at Jax, seething, his gun at his side, then to Ben, the calmer of the two. Surely a minister wouldn't be a part of beating the crap out of him here in the woods, would he? Not that Joe didn't think he deserved a beating. Honestly, he was surprised Jax had waited this long.

But that was it, a few punches? They weren't going to really hurt him, right? At least, he didn't think so.

He looked to Ben for help.

"It would probably be better if you just listened for a while," Ben said, looking calm as could be, like he took part in dragging people off into the woods all the time, which seemed quite unminister-like to Joe.

Kate had said her new husband had a way of making things happen. Surely she hadn't meant this.

"This is the way it is," Ben said, smiling a bit while Jax scowled. "Kate isn't happy."

Joe puzzled over that. He hadn't done anything to Kate, either. Had barely spoken to her, hadn't gotten anywhere near her, and if Kate wasn't happy, wasn't that more Ben's problem than Joe's, given the fact that Ben was her husband now?

"Well, she would be happy—perfectly happy—married to me," Ben said. "Except for one thing."

Joe could just imagine what that one thing was.

"And Kim's not happy," Jax said. "Most important of all to you, I'm not happy, and I could hurt you so easily."

Ben stepped between them at that point. "And if my wife and her family aren't happy, of course I'm not happy," he said.

Okay. Joe hadn't gotten anywhere near any of them, either, but he nodded, to show that he was listening and taking it all in.

"We couldn't possibly be happy right now because a member of our family isn't here," Jax said.

"Okay," Joe said hesitantly.

Kathie. She'd taken off the day of Kate and Ben's wedding, just disappearing after the ceremony. It had been weeks before they'd even known where she was, teaching at some expensive boarding school in North Carolina and resisting all their efforts to get her to come back home.

Joe couldn't blame her. He'd have liked to run away, too, but he wasn't the type to run. He had obligations, and he'd decided to tough it out here, thinking that years of being responsible, dependable, good-guy Joe would overcome a few moments of insanity with his then-fiancé's sister.

But no. Apparently, he was going to be punished for this forever.

And now, they were all mad at him because Kathie wasn't here?

Joe was afraid to have her within a hundred miles of him, afraid of what he might do next to screw up his life, but they wouldn't care about that.

"And since you made this mess," Jax said, glowering down at him, "you are going to fix it."

Joe swallowed hard, bracing himself for a fist to the jaw, wondering if he'd be eating through a straw for the next six weeks because he had no teeth left or because his jaw would be wired shut.

Ouch.

He braced himself as best he could, but Jax didn't hit him.

He just said, "You are going to bring our sister home."

"Me?" Joe said. "But…she hates me."

"That's your problem," Jax said.

"What he means is…we're sure you can find a way around that," Ben said, like all Joe needed to do was turn left instead of right, to get out of a traffic jam.

Women were nothing like traffic jams.

There was no road map, no real signals to tell a man when to stop and when to go ahead. You couldn't call AAA and get a TripTik to tell you to go left for eighty-seven miles and then head north for thirty-seven and then take three right turns and you were there.

"She won't even talk to me," he tried. How could he convince her to come home when she wouldn't even talk to him?

"We're going to leave that problem up to you, too," Ben said, slapping him on the back like they were buddies or something.

"But… I…"

Jax slapped a paper against his chest, and Joe grabbed onto it.

"That's her address. Don't bother to call. Like you said, she wouldn't talk to you anyway. You need to just show up. We included directions. It's only a four-hour drive. Tomorrow's graduation day at that fancy school of hers. She'll be free to do anything she likes once that's over. You're going to go home, pack a bag and start driving."

"Tonight? You want me to go get her tonight?"

"I expect you to be out of town within the hour. And you know I'll know if you're not," Jax said. "I bet you can imagine what's going to happen if anyone catches you here after eight o'clock."

Oh, yeah.

Jax and his buddies on the police force.

Joe had been cited for five moving violations within a week of Kathie leaving town, and he hadn't been guilty of a one. But he hadn't protested, either. Not until he'd ended up before a judge who was ready to take his license away, and then, he hadn't had to say much. The judge had known exactly what was going on and let him off with a warning, specifically that he should try hard to undo whatever he'd done to upset Magnolia Falls' finest.

"Do you have any idea what those tickets did to my insurance rates?" Joe complained.

"Could you possibly think I care?" Jax shot back.

"She won't come back because I ask her to," Joe said in all honesty.

"Then you've got some thinking to do, don't you?" Ben said. "Good thing it's a four-hour drive. I'm sure by the time you get there, you'll have figured out just what to say to get her to come back."

"I can't. I mean... I don't know what to say. I don't think there's anything I can say. If there was, I'd say it." Not because he wanted her to come back...not really. What kind of man welcomed insanity back into his life?

But this was her home, the only one she'd ever known. Her father had died when she was five, her mother last year, and her sisters and brother were all the family she had left. They'd always been tight, and he hated thinking of her cut off from her family this way and all alone in the world, especially if she was upset.

And poor Kate. She'd been like a second mother to her two younger sisters, had always taken very seriously her obligations to them.

He really owed Kate.

And Kathie. He kept thinking of her as a teenager. He'd known her that long, but she was twenty-four now. He'd just turned thirty-one, a grown-up, supposedly a responsible, intelligent one, and he'd handled the whole thing between them so badly.

So he owed them both, and he'd been raised to believe that first, a man tried hard not to make mistakes, and if he did, he always tried to make up for those mistakes.

"Okay," he said, resigned to it but having no idea how he'd accomplish the task of bringing her home. "I'll go."

Which meant, within the next twenty-four hours, Joe would be face-to-face with Kathie Cassidy.

God help him.

Kathie was working at a snotty boys' school in the middle of nowhere. Joe drove into the woods for miles, thinking that surely he was going to end up at a summer camp, but then, there it was, something that looked like an ancient college campus of weathered stone covered in climbing ivy set in the middle of the forest. Odd place for a school, he thought. Jacobsen Hall, the sign had said, full of self-restrained grandeur, the kind that practically screamed old money.

He consulted his directions and found the dorm where she'd been living, serving as a kind of housemother.

Housemother?

Kathie was twenty-four.

Housemothers were not twenty-four.

There was a steady stream of boys and luggage exiting the front door, aided quite often by chauffeurs piling the boys' belongings into limousines.

Okay.

Kathie had talked about teaching in the inner city someday. Jacobsen Hall was as far from that as she could get.

Joe dodged luggage and snotty-looking boys to make his way inside. There in the foyer, clipboard in hand, her blond hair piled on her head in a very prim knot, looking as schoolmarmish as could be, stood Kathie.

He was dismayed to feel a little kick in the gut at the sight of her, even in that little black dress with its little white collar and cuffs.

For one outlandish second, he thought if the skirt was a little shorter and she wore a little white apron, unbuttoned a few of those neat brass buttons and took her hair down, she'd look like…like….

Joe gave an anguished groan.

He was not going to be fantasizing about her.

Under no circumstances would he be having any remotely sexual thoughts about her. None. Never.

He wasn't going insane again for his ex-fiancé's little sister.

No.

He might as well shoot himself right now than go there again.

He just needed a woman. A sane, sensible, practical, responsible, dependable woman. All the things he'd always thought Kate was. All the things he'd always been. And he would settle down with her and have a sane, sensible, practical, responsible, dependable life. He would become his old self. Everyone would forget about the little incident six months ago that had so besmirched his reputation.

There.

He knew what he had to do.

And he could get started on that plan, right after he convinced Kathie to go back home to Magnolia Falls, so her brother and brother-in-law wouldn't beat the crap out of him or have him thrown in jail.

That's all he needed to do.

And stay away from her and have no impure thoughts about her, once she got back there.

Joe didn't feel at all confident about the staying-away part or the lack-of-impure thoughts part, not after he'd been mentally redoing her outfit to make her look like a naughty French maid within moments of seeing her again.

But he couldn't go back to town without her. He'd lose all his teeth.

Not that it was wholly the threat that kept him from turning around and leaving. He owed her. She belonged back there with her family, and he was not going to be the one who ruined her life by taking her away from them, impure thoughts or no impure thoughts.

You're a man. Act like one, he told himself quite sternly.

He marched over to her, his mind firmly on his mission.

She looked up, spotted him and whimpered like a frightened animal.

Honest to God, did she think he was the lowest creature on earth? That she had something to fear from him?

She turned pale. Her hands started to shake, and she looked for a moment like she was going to turn tail and run, like he'd have to chase her. But she finally decided to stand her ground, drawing herself up taller, her chin coming up, a look of embarrassment—and maybe disgust—in her pretty brown eyes.

"Hi, Kathie," he said, shoving his hands into his pockets and wondering if she was going to hit him, thinking he probably deserved it.

She didn't.

She just glared at him. "What are you doing here?"

"I came to see you," he said.

"How did you find me?" she demanded.

"Your brother."

"He would never tell you where I was," she insisted.

Joe pulled out the sheet that contained a little map and directions Jax had printed off the web, along with a scribbled note from Jax that had the name of Kathie's dorm and held it up for her to see.

She made a face, and he could just imagine the phone call Jax was going to get about this if Joe didn't manage to drag her back home, at which point she and her brother could have the conversation in person.

"I have nothing to say to you," she said, crossing her arms in front of her and doing her best to look stubborn, something that had his mouth twitching, trying to hold back a smile.

She was not a stubborn woman. She couldn't be intimidating if she tried, and the only reason he would ever be scared of her was in thinking about his own temporary insanity which he blamed on her.

Which reminded him, he was trying to make up for that.

Which meant, he had to make her listen to him and come back home.

No time for Mr. Nice Guy, not that she'd ever believe that of him again.

"Well, I have something to say to you," he said. "And you're going to listen."

That's how Jax would have treated a woman, right?

Maybe not. Jax would have charmed her into it, but Joe had always felt he lacked in the charm department.

So how the hell was he supposed to manage this?

She gaped at him, no doubt surprised by both his tone and his words, and then she looked hurt, maybe a little teary.

Oh, hell. He'd blown it already.

"Okay, just…listen to me, please?"

She shook her head. "I can't. I can't talk to you. I don't want to see you. Just leave me alone!"

Her voice rose at the end. They were attracting attention. Two of the boys were standing halfway across the room staring in what could only be delight, and one of the other adults, a woman dressed as primly as Kathie, came rushing toward them.

"Kathie? Are you all right?"

Kathie nodded, her lower lip trembling, eyes glistening with unshed tears.

Oh, great, Joe thought.

He was going to be the bad guy again.

"I am not a bad guy!" he said.

Her friend gave him a look that said, *Yeah, right!*

"No, he's not," Kathie said, jumping to his defense.

Which thoroughly puzzled him. If he wasn't the bad guy, who was? He was the only guy involved in the whole situation, which had gone horribly wrong, so he had to be the bad guy, didn't he?

He started to ask, but Kathie didn't give him a chance. She handed her clipboard to her friend and said, "Sign the boys out for me, okay? I have to talk to Joe." Then grabbed him by the hand and started dragging him across the room.

"Joe?" her friend called out. "That's Joe?"

So, he was famous at Jacobsen Hall.

Great.

"Come on," Kathie said, reaching for a door. "In here. Now."

He went without argument, dismayed to find himself alone with her in an empty office. She closed the door behind them, then stood with her back pressed against it, like she didn't want to get too far from it because she might want to flee at any second.

This was going really well.

"You might as well sit down," she said, motioning to an armchair in front of the desk.

Trying to be cooperative and not a bad guy, he sat.

She stood there breathing hard and looking pained. "Okay, what do you want?"

Oh, geez.

He really was no good at this. He was supposed to have figured out how he was going to handle this before he got to this point with her.

"Your family wants you to come back home," he said.

She laughed. "No way. I can't go back there."

"Sure you can. Your whole family's there. They all want you home, Kathie."

"I doubt that."

"Of course they do. They love you. They're miserable without you."

"They were miserable with me. You and I made them miserable."

"Well…they're over it," he said.

It was true, wasn't it?

Not over being mad at him, but certainly over being mad at her.

"They could not possibly be over it," she insisted.

"Sure they are. Call them. They'll tell you."

"I can't talk to them," she said, like he was an idiot for thinking she could.

"Of course you can."

"Joe…what we did…it was awful. It was horrible! I'm so ashamed of myself that I couldn't stand to face them. That's why I had to get away."

"Okay," he said. "I get that. But you've been gone for six months. Believe me, they're all over being mad at you. I mean…they weren't even that mad at you to start with. They're mad at me. Everybody is. You don't have anything to worry about. Everybody in town blames me."

She looked horrified at that.

What? What had he said? He ran through it again in his head.

Everybody in town blames me.

Okay, maybe that was a bad thing to tell her, but it was true.

"That's terrible," she said.

"Well…" What could he say to that? "Not really."

It was uncomfortable and annoying and frustrating, but not awful.

"No, it is. It's not fair at all," she said. "It was me. I was the one. It was my fault."

"No, it wasn't," he claimed. So what if he thought she'd bewitched him or something. He was a grown man, responsible for his own actions. He wasn't going to blame this on her.

"It was. Oh, God, I feel even worse now! They all blame you?"

Joe puzzled over that. It wasn't at all what he had intended to say, but at least she was listening to him. They were having a conversation, and she didn't look like she was going to run away any minute or cry.

Jax had said to do anything it took to get her back. Joe knew this wasn't what he meant, but he was starting to think it was the one thing that might actually work. He knew her, knew how her mind worked and how kindhearted she was. It would be much easier to get her to come back in order to help someone else out of a jam than to help herself.

"Okay, yeah, it's been awful," he said, watching her face as he did. *Oh, yeah. This would work.* "The way you ran away like that. They all thought I must have just been…toying with you, which made what I did even worse."

As if he'd ever been one to toy with women. Her brother toyed with women. Joe did not.

"But, it wasn't like that," she insisted.

He didn't argue that it had been very much like that, just went on, spinning things any way he could to make it most likely that guilt would bring her back.

"And then, when everyone found out about you and me, and then you left…they all thought I dumped you." Had he dumped her? He supposed it could have looked like that as he tried to keep his distance and not make anything worse, tried to not do another stupid thing and kept hoping the whole thing would just blow over. "Everybody thought I was so awful to you, you couldn't even stand to be in the same town with me."

Joe decided it sounded remotely plausible and potentially highly guilt-inducing on her part.

Enough to make her come back?

He hoped so.

Joe figured once he got her back, it was up to Jax and his sisters to keep her there. They hadn't said anything about him having to keep her there, just to get her there.

"But everyone in town loves you," Kathie said.

"Not anymore." He tried to look devastated by that, even if he was more mad than anything else.

Was it working?

"But it wasn't your fault. It was my fault. All of it!"

It wasn't. He knew it wasn't. He'd kissed her. More than once. While he was engaged to her sister, someone she loved and he loved, too.

But if Kathie thought it was her fault, then she'd think it was up to her to fix it, and she couldn't do that from here. She could only do that from Magnolia Falls.

Jax would kill him if he ever found out what Joe said and Joe might dislike himself a little bit more for saying it, but he was with Jax and her family on this—she needed to come home. It was where she belonged, where everyone she loved and who loved her was, and that wasn't something to walk away from in this world. Life was hard enough without people on your side.

"Hey, don't worry about it," he said, still trying to look devastated. "People will get over it. I'm sure of it. And it's not like the bank's business is suffering or anything because of it. Not really—"

"It's hurting the bank's business?" she asked.

"Did I say that? No. Not really."

"Yes, you did. It must be."

He shrugged. "We'll be fine. Don't worry about it. Some new scandal will hit town, and everybody will forget about how awful I was to you and Kate."

Kate.

That gave him another idea.

He knew she loved her sister.

"And I don't think anyone really believes Kate's so mad at you that she can't forgive you," he added on a whim. "Or that silly rumor about her ordering you to leave town and never come back!"

"They think she threw me out of town?"

"No. I don't think anyone really believes that. They know Kate. They know she'd never do that. The idea that she had you stand up for her at the wedding, so she wouldn't look so bad, and then turned around right afterward and ran you out of town…that's just silly. Forget I even said it."

Kathie looked horrified. "I never thought of them blaming you and Kate."

"And don't think of it now. Really. We're fine. We'll weather this. It'll just take some time."

"It's not right," Kathie insisted.

"It's fine," he said again.

"No, it's not. And I can't let this happen. I have to do something."

"Well…if you really want to help—"

"What? Tell me what to do?"

"I think if you came back for the summer and saw Kate, it would show everyone that those silly things people are saying about Kate not forgiving you and running you out of town…that would be over. Everyone would know it wasn't true."

"Yes, they would." Kathie squared her shoulders, looking determined and very, very sad. "And you. I can't have them thinking you're to blame for all of this. I'll have to spend some time with Kate, and then I'll have to spend some time with you."

No, no, no, Joe thought.

Not him.

Not him and her.

No.

That was not part of the plan.

"I'm fine," he insisted.

"No, I have to make this right. They think you…that you and I…while you were engaged to Kate?" She couldn't even say it. "And then when she found out about us, you dumped me?"

Joe nodded, thinking this was bad. It was going to be so bad.

"No wonder they hate you," she said, then looked dismayed. "Joe, we have to convince them that you didn't dump me."

"No, we don't."

"Yes, we do. I could just tell them I dumped you. I could just tell Melanie Mann, that girl Kate went to school with, the one who was spreading all the rumors about Kate last fall. She'd tell the whole town in no time. That's it. I'll tell Melanie I dumped you."

"Okay," Joe said, thinking it was time to say goodbye to his teeth. Jax would despise any plan that involved making Kathie look bad, and he wouldn't take it sitting down.

How bad would it be living on little cans of Ensure, the thing old people drank, because they could suck it up through a straw, no teeth needed? He had a second cousin who broke nearly every bone in his face in a car accident and lived on Ensure for months. He'd made it. Surely Joe could, too.

"And if that doesn't work, we'll just have to be seen together again," Kathie said, looking as miserable about the idea as Joe was.

Just shoot me now, Joe thought.

He'd made a fool of himself over her.

A complete fool.

Undone years of careful, respectable living, all in a few stolen moments with her.

"Yeah, that's what we'll do," Kathie said. "We'll...you know...be seen together, like we are together, just a few times, and a few weeks later, I'll dump you. I'll just say I'm done with you, and you can claim you're heartbroken, and everyone will feel sorry for you and be nice to you again."

Joe groaned.

Oh, hell.

Jax had said to get her back home.

And it sounded like Joe had convinced her to come back.

So why was he certain things were about to get worse instead of better?

Maybe he'd break his own jaw, just to save time.

Chapter Two

Kathie threw her things into two suitcases while her friend Liz peered out the door to see where Joe was.

"Yep, still there," she said, closing the door and then grinning. "And he's kind of cute, in that clean-cut, not-a-wrinkle-in-sight, not-a-brown-hair-out-of-place kind of way."

He was gorgeous, Kathie thought, but then she wasn't going to let herself think that. He was never wrinkled or messy, never had a hair out of place and never looked anything but solid, dependable and completely capable of handling anything that might come along. Everything a man should be and that a woman could count on, and Kathie had thought so for too many years to deny it, at least to herself.

"I'm telling you," Liz said, "a man doesn't come all this way to get a woman to come back to him, if he's not interested in her."

"He's not interested in me," she insisted.

"Sure he is. You didn't see the way he looked at you. Even in these ridiculous schoolmarm getups they make us wear. I mean, if a man can be interested in a woman wearing this…"

"He's not interested. He never has been, and he never will be," Kathie insisted.

"So…all that stuff that happened last year—"

"It wasn't all that stuff," she insisted, shoving two sweaters and a pair of hiking boots into her suitcase. "It was a few kisses. A few hugs, and a lot of guilt. That was it. And he didn't kiss me. I kissed him, and now everybody is blaming him for it. It's terrible."

"Wait a minute. He came up here to get you to come back because everyone's blaming him for what happened? He said that to you?"

"He didn't mean to," Kathie said, reaching for her CD collection and the earrings her mother had left her. "I could tell he didn't mean to. It just slipped out."

"So, why did he come to see you?"

"Because he's a nice guy—"

"Who got caught making out with his fiancé's sister? This is not the way a nice guy acts," Liz insisted.

"He is a nice guy. He just… I just… I practically attacked him!"

Liz laughed. "No way. You wouldn't know how to attack a guy, even if you wanted to, not that I can imagine you wanting to. You don't have an attack-the-opposite-sex bone in your body."

"I do where he's concerned!"

Liz gasped. "You still want him?"

"I do not," Kathie lied, her face flaming. *Dammit.*

Liz gasped again. "You do! You swore it was nothing. A schoolgirl crush gone mad, coupled with the grief over losing your mother."

"It was. That's what it was." The first time she'd kissed him was the day her mother died. She'd been crying hopelessly one minute and in his arms the next. "I still don't even know how it happened."

Honestly, she didn't.

"How old were you when you met him?" Liz asked.

"Just turned nineteen," Kathie whispered.

Nineteen and never really been in love before. Never even been close. It was insane. Girls all around her, all through high school had fallen in love every time they turned around. She kept waiting for it to happen to her, and it never did. Not back then.

But her older sister had come home from college where she'd met a guy. Kate brought him home, and Kathie had taken one look and felt like she couldn't breathe, couldn't see anyone but him.

She'd told herself it was crazy, that she'd get over it, outgrow it, but she never had.

It had been her guilty secret for the five long years in which Kate and Joe had been engaged. Years in which everyone had agreed that they were perfect for each other. She had tormented herself over that man and maintained a façade of easy friendship and nothing more, until she'd thrown herself into his arms the day her mother died.

And then…everything just went crazy.

He'd broken it off with her sister, or maybe Kate had broken it off with him. Kathie had never been sure and she'd heard several different versions of the story. Rumors had been flying all over town.

Almost at the same instant, Kate met Ben, and then, to everyone's amazement, fell for him completely and married him, and in the middle of that, she'd found out about Kathie and Joe. Kathie had been horrified. The moment the wedding was over, she'd run away and hadn't come back. She couldn't bring herself to face her family or Joe.

"Oh, honey, you've got it bad for the man," Liz said, coming to Kathie's side and giving her a hug.

"I don't. I can't. I have to forget about him—"

"Why? He hasn't forgotten about you."

"He feels guilty about what happened. That's all. He loved my sister. He's always loved my sister, and he lost her, because of me!"

"Because he confessed that he had feelings for another woman while he was engaged to your sister, and the other woman was you."

"Feelings?" Kathie said, trying to shove five books and a plant in her suitcase. Okay, the plant was a lost cause. It would not go. She set it on the windowsill, where it had lived for the past four months, and tried not to cry again. "Guilt is a feeling, and believe me, guilt is the only thing he feels for me. He's an honorable man who's loved my sister forever, and then... everything just got all messed up. I messed it all up."

"Yeah, but if he really cared about you—"

"He doesn't. If he did, he would have said so, but he didn't. He looked me right in the eye at Kate's wedding, when everybody knew the whole story and everyone was watching us and whispering about us, and do you know what he told me?"

"What?"

"That he was sorry. Not that he cared about me, but that he was sorry about everything that had happened, that it was all his fault, but it wasn't all his fault. It was mine. I knew it. He was just trying to be nice about it by saying it was his fault, because he's a nice guy."

"Who has a thing for you," Liz insisted. "And you have a major thing for him."

"I can't. He can't. We can't. Too many people have been hurt by this. I'm trying to fix it now, not start something all over again."

"I think you want to see him again," Liz said.

"No. Really. I don't."

She wanted her life back, her nice, quiet, careful, never-done-anything-wrong life with her family who loved her and no one in town who ever gossiped about her and no rumors flying about her and her sister's fiancé. Nothing to be ashamed about. No reason to run away.

That's what she wanted.

Really.

Not Joe Reed.

"I just need to see my family," she said.

"And what are you going to say to them?"

"I have no idea."

Joe waited until her things were packed, carried her suitcases to her car, a cute little bright yellow Volkswagen bug, and then said he'd follow her.

"All the way back to Magnolia Falls?" she asked.

"Yes," he said, opening the door to his banker's car, a sedate black four-door sedan.

"Why? You don't trust me to really go back there?"

"Well…" he hedged, standing in the bright sunshine filtering down through the trees. "No. Not that. I just… I mean, we're both going to the same place, right? We might as well drive together."

"I'm twenty-four years old, Joe. I can find my way back to town by myself," she insisted.

"Of course. I know that. I just…"

"Don't trust me to actually come back. What do

you think? I'm going to stand here and tell you I will, and then take off in the other direction? You think I'm a liar and a coward?"

"No. Really, I don't," he said, closing his car door and coming over to her, where she didn't want him, not anywhere near her. "I just think it was a bad situation, and I'm sorry, about everything, and I know how important it is to your family to have you back, so…"

Not to him. To her family. Just as she suspected. He probably hadn't given her a second thought, not in the way she wished he would.

"And what about you? With everything that happened, I mean?" she asked, before he could think she was asking about him and her. "Let's say, with Kate being married. How are you with that?"

"I hope she's happy," he said, and seemed to mean it.

Could he possibly? He'd been crazy about her sister since the moment she'd met him. He'd followed her back to Magnolia Falls after graduation, taken a job at the local bank and settled down there, becoming as much a part of the town as Kathie and her siblings, who had been born there. His mother had left some silly retirement village someplace near Atlanta to go there, and when it had been time to move his grandmother into a nursing home, they'd brought her to Magnolia Falls, too. This was a man who'd been sure of himself and his future with her sister.

"Kate seems really happy with Ben," Joe added. "I see them around town every now and then. I just ran into Ben yesterday, at the town picnic, as a matter of fact."

Which meant…what? That they were buddies now? That it didn't hurt at all, thinking about Kate married to someone else?

Kathie stared at the face of the man she'd dreamed about for years and couldn't detect the first hint of what was going on inside of him. That was one thing about Joe that had always kept her guessing. He wasn't a man to show easily how he felt. He could be dying inside, and she wasn't sure she'd ever know it.

Was that how he felt now? Like he was dying inside?

Or was he over the whole thing?

Kathie didn't see how that could be possible. Five years together didn't just disappear into a puff of smoke, not what they'd had. They were meant to be together. Everyone had said so. And Kathie had ruined it by throwing herself at Joe and confusing him, until out of guilt, he'd confessed what had happened to Kate.

That was all it had been. Kathie was sure of it. Guilt, confusion and a few stolen kisses.

Not love.

Not anything like that.

And now he stood there in front of her saying

Kate seemed happy and acting like he and Kate's new husband were the best of friends?

No way Kathie was buying that act.

"Are you ready to go?" Joe asked.

"Yes, but there is no way you're following me all the way back home, like I'm sixteen and can't be trusted in a car by myself," she said.

"But—"

"No. No arguments." She wasn't going to be treated like a child. "Go on. I'll see you there."

He followed her!

That infuriating man tried to follow her all the way home. She'd speed up. He'd speed up. She'd slow down, and he would, too, from his spot three cars behind her on the highway.

She finally made it back to the apartment she used to share with her younger sister, Kim, a place she'd been paying rent on for months, even though she wasn't living there, because she wouldn't leave her sister in the lurch like that. Besides, living at the boarding school, she had practically no expenses, so she could afford it. She hadn't done it because she hadn't been able to stand the idea of not having a place to come home to one day. Really, she hadn't.

Kathie parked on the street in front of the big old house now cut up into apartments. Joe pulled in behind her, getting out of his car, slamming the door behind him and stalking over to her side.

"Did you know you were going ninety-one miles an hour back there at one point?" he bellowed. "I didn't think this little thing you drove could go ninety-one miles an hour, but it did."

"What do you mean, Joe? Were you following me or something?" She blinked up at him, as innocently as she could manage, considering the fact that she was furious.

"No," he claimed.

"Oh. You just happened to be three cars behind for the last four hours?"

"I…I just wanted to make sure you got home okay," he said.

She was about to lay into him again when she heard a quick blast of a siren behind her. It was her brother. He pulled in, in his police cruiser, right behind Joe and was out of the car in seconds, grabbing her and hugging her and swinging her around in his arms.

"It's about time you came back home," Jax said, flashing the megawatt grin that had had women falling all over themselves to get to him for more than a decade. "God, I've missed you. We all have. I'm so happy you're home."

She gave him a big hug, once he put her back on her own two feet on the ground. "I missed you, too."

Then she realized he'd just happened to drive down this street at exactly the right moment to find her getting out of her car. Not that it was the first time her big brother had just happened to drive along at exactly the right moment. He'd made a habit of it during her teen years.

Plus, there was something about the look that passed between him and Joe, as Jax said, "We can take it from here, Joe."

"Wait a minute," Kathie said, then turned to her brother. "How did you know the minute I pulled in?"

He shrugged easily. "Just lucky, I guess."

"No, that's not it."

"Okay, I might have had some friends watching for you," he said. "You know me. I'm always watching out for you and Kim, even Kate."

"And you just thought, hey, maybe today of all days, Kathie will come home?"

"Sure," he said, looking a bit less comfortable now.

"No, that's not it. You sent Joe to get me," she said, wishing she could die right then and there on the street, so she would never have to face Joe again. Joe who hadn't come because he'd wanted to or because he'd wanted her back, but because her older brother had twisted his arm, or something to that effect! Joe who'd never really wanted her. How she could have thought he might...

Kathie could have sunk into the ground quite happily at the idea of her thinking that for once, Joe had really wanted her and had come to get her.

"And you!" She turned to Joe, because it was either yell at him or cry, and she really didn't want to cry over him anymore. Not one more tear. "You must have called him and told him the minute I'd be back!"

"Kathie, wait a minute," her brother said. "Joe and I aren't exactly buddies, you know? We don't have a lot to say to each other these days."

She turned to Joe. "Tell me. He sent you, didn't he?"

"I...I was worried about you, Kathie," Joe said, looking very, very guilty.

Oh, God. If it was possible to die of embarrassment, now was the time. Right now. She waited, barely breathing, disappointed to realize she was going to live and that she'd have to face them both.

She laughed, a scary sound even to her own ears, and said, "But Jax is the one who sent you, isn't he? I wouldn't talk to him or come back for him, so he sent you."

"Kathie, everybody wants you back home," her brother insisted.

"How did you make him do it, Jax? How did you make him drive up there and talk me into coming back?"

"Kathie—"

"Tell me," she yelled at both of them. "It's my life. I think I have a right to know!"

"Look, I'm sorry," Joe said. "I wouldn't have

done it if I hadn't known how much they all want you back. They're your family, Kathie. You guys have always been so close, and I know you love them. This is where you should be."

He turned around and left.

Kathie watched him, hot, angry tears filling her eyes.

He had no idea.

She couldn't be here. Not with him here, not loving her, not even thinking about her. She couldn't!

Kathie looked back at her brother, whom she'd been so happy to see just moments ago, and wished she could smack him.

"What did you do?" she asked, sounding weak and weepy, everything she didn't want to be. "Go ahead. I'll get it out of you eventually. You know that. What did you do to get him to come after me?"

"I threatened to break his jaw into sixteen different pieces," Jax said, like it was no big deal, like he threatened people every day.

For all she knew, he did. Maybe that was why he loved his job so much. He got to order people around all the time, just like he had when they were kids. Make him the oldest and the only boy, and then take away their father to a bullet when they were little, and what did you get?

A brother who thought he was in charge of everything.

"I cannot believe you did this!" she yelled, then stood there while every bit of the fight drained out of her and she was so weary, she could hardly breathe.

"Kathie, I—"

He reached for her, but she jerked her arm away and stalked off toward the house, leaving him standing there yelling back at her.

"Oh, come on, Kathie. Was it really so bad? Sending the rat after you? We just wanted you back, that's all, and you wouldn't talk to any of us! Kathie!"

She ran inside the house, up the stairs and got her key in the front door of her apartment, ignoring her brother altogether when he knocked on the door, when he pounded, even when he shouted.

They all wanted her back.

Well, fine. She was back.

It didn't mean she had to talk to them or see them, and it certainly didn't mean she had to stay.

"What did you do?" Kate stared at her new husband, who should know her moods well enough by now to be uneasy about her current state of mind, then at her brother, who definitely knew better, but just did ridiculous things anyway.

"What do you mean, what did we do?" Jax made himself comfortable in her kitchen by grabbing a carton of orange juice out of the fridge and downing what was left in it in practically one gulp. "We got her home. I thought you'd be happy. I thought you'd be jumping for joy, and we'd be heroes."

"That depends. What did you do?" Kate said, crossing her arms and trying out her sternest look on both of them.

Ben was going to play innocent and then try to make her laugh. She could tell. That's what he always did when he annoyed her, and it usually worked, because she adored him, but her brother was a different story altogether.

She and Jax both tended to think they knew what was best for their younger siblings, which had led to any number of clashes over the years. Kate was trying to let go of her controlling tendencies, but Jax's had gotten even worse since their sister took off six months ago and, to date, had adamantly refused to come home, no matter what kind of begging or pleading anyone had done.

"Can you not just be happy?" Jax asked, maybe catching a hint of the trouble he was in, but maybe not. Maybe he was oblivious still. "You know? Wow! Jump up and down. Kiss your husband. Hug your brother. Go see your sister? That kind of happy?"

"Not until I know how you got her back here," Kate said, picking up the knife she'd been using to chop carrots and holding it purposefully in front of her. "What did you say? What finally worked?"

"We didn't say anything," said Ben, doing his Mr. Innocent routine.

"Oh, okay. Neither one of you said a word, and yet, you somehow got her back here," she said, waving the knife a bit for good measure. "Which leads me to my previous question. What did you do?"

"We didn't do anything," Jax claimed. "Joe did it."

"Yeah, Joe did it."

"Joe, who she won't talk to any more than she'll talk to any of us? He got her to come back? Okay, what did Joe do?"

"He didn't say exactly," Jax said, looking to Ben. "Did he?"

"Not to me."

"Right. He didn't say."

"Okay, now I'm really worried," Kate said. "You two have done something, and I'm thinking it didn't turn out the way you'd hoped and now you want me to fix it." She looked pointedly at her brother, whom she was sure was the guilty party.

"No. You've got it all wrong," he claimed. "We just wanted to tell you she was back…so you could go see her. Don't you want to go see her?"

"Yes."

"And you should go now. You could put the knife down and go now," Jax said. "I mean…why not go now? You haven't seen her in months. Why wait?"

"For one thing, I'm in the middle of cooking dinner."

"I'll do it," Ben offered, taking the knife from her before she could object.

"Me, too." Jax jumped in, picking up a container of rice and shaking it. "I can help. Really. What do you do with this?"

"I'm going to start throwing things in five seconds, if you don't tell me what's going on!"

"Okay, okay," her brother said, putting the rice back down. "She might be… a little upset."

Kate arched a brow. "Because…"

"She might be…a little mad," Ben said.

Kate tried again. "What did you two do, kidnap her?"

"No," they insisted.

"Because I know Joe wouldn't kidnap her." He would never force anyone to do anything against their will.

"No, I'm sure it wasn't anything like that," Ben said. "She just…well—"

"Okay, she might be leaving again," Jax said, his expression bland as could be.

Oh, this was bad.

Bad!

"And why would she be leaving, when she just got here?" Kate asked.

"We're not sure," Ben said. "Maybe…because we sent Joe to get her? Was it really that bad? Sending Joe?"

"That depends," Kate said, thinking she could

imagine scenarios in which that would be very, very bad, depending on how her sister now felt about Joe. Then she thought of something else. "Exactly how did you send Joe to get her?"

"We might have...threatened him," Ben said, stripping off his clerical collar as he said it. He always got rid of it when he'd done something decidedly unministerly. "Okay, I didn't threaten him. I swear. You know I don't do that stuff. I just... stood by and advised him to cooperate while your brother threatened him."

"You threatened him?" She yelled at her brother, then turned to her husband. "And you went along with it?"

"Just trying to fit in with the family, you know?" Ben claimed. "Be a part of things? Make you happy, by getting your sister home. That kind of thing. That's all."

Kate wanted to scream, but managed not to, barely.

Poor Kathie.

She'd been through so much in the last fifteen months, starting with losing their beloved mother.

"Let me take a wild guess," Kate said, turning back to her brother. "You threatened Joe that if he didn't go get her and convince her to come back..."

"He'd break his jaw," Ben said, eager to help her understand now.

"Who's breaking someone's jaw?" Shannon,

Kate and Ben's sixteen-year-old, soon-to-be-offi-cially-adopted daughter showed up in the kitchen at just the right moment.

"No one broke anyone's jaw," Ben said.

"Your uncle just threatened to," Kate said.

"Oh." Shannon nodded as she opened the refrig-erator and stuck her head inside. "And they thought I'd be trouble."

"Yeah, who'd have thought the adults would be the ones to make trouble?" Kate said. "Another big guess here…Kathie found out you threatened to break Joe's jaw, and because of that, Joe went to see her and convinced her to come back, right?"

"Yeah," her brother admitted. "Why is that so bad?"

"Ahhhhhh!" Kate did scream then. "People think you know so much about women and that you're so good with them, but it's just crap, Jax. It's complete and total crap!"

Kate knocked three separate times, knowing her sister had to be there, because her car was out front. Who else drove a bright yellow bug with a rainbow sticker on the back and bumper stickers that said, Visualize Whirled Peas and, What Would Jesus Bomb? Kate had missed her sister desperately.

"Kathie, please," Kate called out through the door. "I have dinner on the stove. I'll go home and poison them with it, if it'll make you feel better, promise. Just let me in first."

That did it. The door swung open.

Her poor sister stood there with big red eyes and a thoroughly defeated expression on her face.

"Oh, baby," Kate said, taking her sister in her arms.

"They told you what they did?" Kathie asked.

"It wasn't easy, but I got it out of them."

"And you're willing to hurt them for me?"

"Sure, I will. They've gotten to be buddies, but they're dangerous together. I think Jax has been waiting for years to have another man in the family, you know, so it won't be three against one anymore. And he's going a little nuts waiting for Gwen's mother to get better, so they can have their wedding with her here. Ever since she broke her hip, and Jax and Gwen postponed the wedding, he's been a little…intense."

Kathie nodded, her head still on Kate's shoulder.

Kate gave her a big squeeze. "How about I make them both throw up their dinner? I think I can do that with no problem. I mean… I did it by accident once, trying to impress Ben's mother. Surely I can do it on purpose."

And if anyone at Ben's church heard about it, she'd never live it down.

Oh, well.

She'd tried to tell him she wouldn't quite fit in, but he hadn't listened.

Not that it was going badly. Her and the church ladies, as she called them. Not at all. She just kept expecting it to go badly.

Poisoning her husband would definitely make things go badly, because they all adored him. They thought he was right up there with God.

"Just don't tell anybody, okay? I'm afraid the church ladies are watching all the time, and that they're convinced no one will ever be good enough for Ben," Kate said.

Kathie finally lifted her head and stepped back. She wiped at her tears with the back of her hand and smiled a bit. "So… I missed you."

"Oh, honey, I missed you so much! I didn't think you'd ever come back."

There were more hugs, more tears, and when those finally subsided, Kate had a million things she wanted to say and no idea how to start. All the possibilities seemed fraught with red flags.

Kathie finally started things off. "So…you're okay?"

"I'm great."

"And you're…happy?"

"Yes. Kim's settled right in for her first year of teaching. Shannon is doing so well, and we just saw the baby she gave up for adoption. They named her Elissa, and she's sitting up and babbling and slobbers on everything. Her parents have a two-year-old named Emily, and they invited us all to

Emily's birthday party two weeks ago. Ben is absolutely wonderful, until Jax comes along and talks him into doing something like this. Poor Ben, he wants to fit in so badly, he'll go along with anything Jax says, any scheme he comes up with."

"Well…good," Kathie said like she couldn't quite believe it. "That's good. I'm happy for you, and I just want you to know, I'm here to fix everything."

"Okay." Kate wasn't quite sure what that meant, but she was ready to agree to most anything her sister wanted.

"At least, everything I can fix. I mean, I know it was awful—"

"Kathie, no—"

"It was, and I know that, and I feel just awful about it—"

"I'm not mad, I promise," Kate protested.

"But I'm going to fix as much of it as I can. Joe said people in town think I've stayed away because you can't forgive me for what he and I did, that there's a rumor going around that you threw me out of town."

"Well, that's just silly," Kate said.

"No, it's awful. I can't let people think that about you."

"Kathie, I don't care what anybody thinks anymore. I know I used to, but I'm over it. I care about Ben and my family, and maybe the church ladies, a little bit, just because I want them to like me and think I'm right for Ben, because I know how much they all love him. But that's it, I swear."

"Well, I still don't want anybody to think you kicked me out of town," Kathie said. "So I thought if I just came back for a little while, and people saw us together and happy, they'd know that's not true."

"Okay." That worked for Kate. Anything that got her sister back and had them spending time together, worked for Kate.

"And Joe didn't want to tell me, but...I guess everybody hates him now!"

"Well, I don't know if I'd go that far...."

"Everybody blames him for what happened. Not me. Him. He said they all think he dumped me, after...you know, making trouble between you and him, and you and me. That he dumped me when everybody found out about it, and I was so devastated, I left town."

"I guess it's possible. I don't know. Honestly, I've heard every rumor in the world about the whole thing, and I just try not to listen anymore." Kate would have said again it didn't matter to her, but like her brother, she wanted her sister to come back to stay.

She wasn't going to be as bad as her brother, was she?

No jaw breaking and no threats, but still as bad in her own way. Like being ready to let her sister believe anything to keep Kathie here?

"It wasn't Joe's fault," Kathie insisted. "Honest, it wasn't. It was me. All of it was me."

Kate didn't believe that for a second. After thinking about it for a long, long time, she chose to believe that two of the people she knew best in the world had, completely unexpectedly, developed real feelings for each other, which might have been a real problem for her if, in the middle of the whole thing, she hadn't found the love of her life.

So whatever had happened between her sister and her ex-fiancé was completely okay with her now. She just couldn't seem to convince Kathie of that, no matter how hard she tried. Mostly, Kathie wouldn't even let her bring up the subject. She wanted her sister here, and she wanted her happy, and one thing Kate had figured out was that Kathie and Joe both seemed miserable without each other.

Which wasn't okay with Kate at all.

So, Kathie was worried about people blaming and hating Joe for whatever had happened between the two of them?

"Well...I don't know what you can do about that," Kate said carefully, in case there was something and it was something that would keep her sister in town, where she belonged.

"That's why I came back," her sister said. "To show everybody that you're not mad at me and that you didn't kick me out of town."

"Okay," Kate said. That was fine with her. That was very good.

"And to show everybody that Joe didn't dump me," Kate said. "I dumped him."

"You dumped him?" Kate asked. Why would her sister dump Joe, if Joe was the one she truly wanted?

"Okay, I didn't really dump him. I mean, he was never mine to dump. He and I were just…" Kathie's face turned beet red. "I don't know what we were. Stupid, I guess. I was just stupid and selfish and confused, and once everyone found out last fall, I just couldn't stand to be here, with everybody knowing and talking about us. So, I have a plan."

Kate nodded very carefully. "What plan?"

"If it's okay with you, I mean, I'm going to pretend to see Joe for a few weeks…."

Her sister waited…for Kate to object? "Okay," Kate said.

"And then I'm going to dump him, so people won't blame him for the whole thing anymore. So he won't be the bad guy."

"Joe asked you to come back to town to pretend to date him, then dump him, so that people would stop blaming him for dumping you?" Kate asked.

"No! He would never do that. I don't think he even meant to tell me. It just slipped out, but once I knew, I had to try to fix things, because it wasn't right for people to blame you and him when it was all my fault," her sister explained.

Okay.

That kind of made sense, but only because Kate knew her sister so well.

Joe had been threatened within an inch of his life and forced to go see Kathie, and then, when he tried to talk her into coming back, as ordered, something had gone wrong, and he'd ended up giving her the impression that everyone in town blamed Joe and Kate for Kathie's decision to leave, and Kathie was here to make sure everyone blamed her instead?

Not what Joe intended, Kate was sure, but it had gotten her sister to come back. Once Kathie saw a problem that she believed she'd created, she wouldn't give up until she fixed things.

And Kathie could only fix things from here in town.

Kate weighed her options carefully. If she protested that she wasn't mad at her sister at all, that it was fine with her if Kathie and Joe fell madly in love, and that she didn't care what anyone in town thought of any of that, Kathie might not stay and try to fix things.

And she really wanted Kathie to stay, no matter what the reason.

Maybe Kate was as bad as her brother.

"Well…that sounds like a good plan," Kate said, feeling guilty about it but happy. It sounded like a plan that would keep her sister in town for weeks at least, forever if Kate had anything to say about it.

"Still mad?" Ben asked, coming up behind Kate in the kitchen and putting his arms around her.

"Maybe."

He kissed her cheek, then nuzzled her neck. "Come on. It wasn't so bad, was it?"

"Only if she's in love with him," Kate said.

"In love with him?" Ben turned her around in his arms.

"Yes," Kate said, letting him draw her against him, her head tucked against his chest. "Think about it. She's in love with him, and he just let her leave after our wedding. Probably because his head was still spinning from everything that had happened and because he was still trying to make sense of it and failing miserably. Joe doesn't change his mind easily. He doesn't change his plans, either. It would take him some time to figure everything out, and she left so fast, thinking he didn't care about her at all, that it was some crazy fluke."

"Okay, but—"

"I don't think it was a fluke to Kathie. I think she's in love with him, and now look what's happened. Her brother and her new brother-in-law went to the man she loves, who she thinks doesn't love her, and threatened to break his jaw if he didn't go see her and get her to come back to town."

"But...if she's in love with him, doesn't she want to see him again?"

"Not if she thinks it's hopeless and the only reason he came to get her is because he didn't want his jaw broken into sixteen pieces. Then, it's just humiliating to have to be here with him, thinking he couldn't care less about her."

"Oh. Okay. I get it now."

Yes, now, he got it.

Poor Kathie.

Chapter Three

Kathie's younger sister, Kim, threw open the door and squealed when she got home from a late day at school and saw Kathie standing there. The next thing Kathie knew, they were in each other's arms. Kim was practically bouncing with joy and squeezing her so tight.

Kathie was so relieved she nearly cried right then and there.

"I can't believe it!" Kim said over and over again. "I didn't think you'd ever come back."

Then Kim was almost crying, too.

"Really. Not ever. The longer you stayed away, the more worried I got. I didn't think we'd all ever be together again, and I couldn't stand that idea. I just couldn't stand it!"

"I know," Kathie said, her bottom lip trembling.

It had been the worst thing. The absolute worst, right after thinking they all must hate her for what she'd done to her beloved older sister. Thinking that they'd never be a family again, the way they always had been. That she'd be completely cut off from them, and that it was something she deserved…it had been horrible.

She feared she still deserved it, but couldn't help but think it was so incredibly wonderful to be home, no matter what the circumstances.

"So, it's all over, right?" Kim asked, nearly begging. "You're back. To stay. Right?"

"I don't know," Kathie said, watching her sister's face fall into disbelief.

She hadn't thought about this—about how hard it would be on Kim to have her back and think everything would go back to normal, when all Kathie was doing was trying to fix the mess she'd made as best she could and then disappear again.

"What do you mean, you don't know? This town is your home. This is where you belong!"

"I know. I just…I've never really lived anywhere else, except when I was at college," Kathie tried. She'd never been the adventurous sort. She was the quiet one. Jax was the charmer. Kate, the smart one, and Kim the beauty. Kathie was the mouse. All she'd ever wanted was to feel safe, right here in Magnolia Falls, in the midst of her loving family, but she had to say something to try to explain herself. "I mean, there's a whole world out there. You know that. You love to travel. There might be all sorts of places I'd love to live."

Kim looked unconvinced. She looked hurt, and maybe even mad. Kim who was never mad at her.

"I have to try, you know?"

"No. I don't know," Kim complained. "Don't you love us anymore? Don't you miss us?"

"Of course, I do."

"You're supposed to be getting over everything," Kim argued. "So that everything can get back to normal."

"I want that," Kathie insisted.

Oh, God, she wanted it.

She just didn't think it was possible.

"It was awful when you left," her sister said, sitting down on the sofa. "Terrible. It was the worst thing. Mom was gone, and then you were gone, and I just kept thinking, who's going to disappear next? For months, everybody else kept saying you were bound to come home soon, that you wouldn't be able to stay away. Not me. I kept thinking, who's going to leave next?"

"Oh, Kimmie. I'm so sorry!"

One more thing to add to her list of sins against her family.

She took her sister into her arms and held on tight.

Kimmie had been a baby when their father died. She had no memories of him at all, just pictures and the stories they all told her about him. And she'd still been in college when their mother died. Because she was so young, Kathie and her brother and sister had tried harder for Kim than anyone else to make sure she felt safe and secure, a part of a strong, loving family.

But Kathie had just left, not even thinking of how her younger sister would feel about it. Kathie had thought she was trying to save the rest of them by leaving. But Kim just saw it as losing one more person in an ever-dwindling family circle.

Kathie had done even more damage than she thought.

Kim hardly spoke to her the rest of the night. She went to bed early, got up early and left. The school year still wasn't over in Magnolia Falls, and Kim taught art at the elementary school.

Kathie hid in their apartment for three solid hours, then had to call herself all forms of the word coward just to get herself to go outside and risk seeing anyone she knew.

It was spring in Magnolia Falls, warm and sunny, very, very green, everything smelling fresh and new.

If only Kathie could have started all over again, just wound back the clock, what would she do?

Never fall for Joe. Never have some silly, schoolgirl crush in the first place or have it and get over it, completely, ages ago, like other girls did, so that no one would ever be hurt or ever have to know.

But she couldn't do that.

Which meant she had to do the next best thing.

She had to fix this as best she could. Make people see that it wasn't his fault, and it wasn't her sister's. Move on with the plan, and then get away from here again, even if it killed her this time.

She'd taken the time to fix her hair, put on a bit of makeup and dress in her favorite jeans and a bright yellow top, trying to look as good as she could and not have anyone guess how terrible she felt, how scared, how ashamed, how sad.

She was going to march into the center of town, into the bank where Joe worked and go to lunch with him, in full sight of everyone there, on the street and in the Corner Café, a hotbed of gossip dead-center in town.

Time to get moving with the Joe-didn't-dump-Kathie-and-Joe-isn't-the-bad-guy plan.

Which meant she had to look happy to see him, and he had to look happy to see her. Kathie was afraid that might be a problem, so she pulled out her cell phone and called the bank, asking for him.

"May I say who's calling?" the receptionist asked politely.

Kathie was pretty sure it was Stacy Morganstern, who used to be on the same peewee football cheerleading squad as Kim.

"Stacy? It's Kathie."

Stacy gasped. "Kathie Cassidy?"

"Yes."

"You're back in town? I hadn't heard!"

"Just got in last night," Kathie said. "How are you?"

"Well…fine. Just fine. How are you?"

"Great."

"Where have you been? Everyone was so worried, and then no one knew, and—"

"Teaching. I was teaching. A temporary position in North Carolina, but it's over now. Joe brought me home yesterday."

"Joe?" Stacy gasped once more.

"Yes. He drove up and helped me move." Not entirely untrue. He'd carried her suitcases to her car, after all.

"You've been seeing Joe? All this time?"

No way to answer that without lying, which Kathie really didn't like to do.

"Stacy, I'm sorry. I'm kind of in a rush. I want to catch Joe before he makes lunch plans. Could you put me through?"

"Oh. Okay. Sure. I'll get him for you."

Kathie breathed a bit easier after escaping from the you've-been-seeing-Joe question. Relief was still rushing through her when Joe came on the phone.

"Kathie?" He sounded like a man approaching a rabid dog.

God, help me, please. I won't ever go after my sister's fiancé again. I swear. I won't fall for any man I'm not allowed to have.

"We need to have lunch together," she said in a rush, not giving herself time to think about it.

Just do it.

Follow the plan.

The Joe-is-not-the-bad-guy plan.

"Okay," he said, still sounding like she might bite his head off or something.

"I mean, if we're going to do this, we just have to do it. Which means, people have to see us together."

"Okay," Joe said. "I'll pick you up in a half hour?"

"No, I'll meet you at the bank. It's always crowded at noon. Might as well start there, letting people see us, and then we'll go to the Corner Café."

Joe groaned. "You mean the diner?"

"Yes."

"Darlene remodeled and changed the name. It's actually called the Corner Diner now and it's bigger."

His chance meeting with Kate at the Corner Diner last fall was still probably the talk of the town, the best gossip to come out of the place in years. They'd run into each other in the midst of breaking up, and Kate had informed Joe very loudly that no, despite gossip to the contrary, she was not pregnant with his child or anyone else's. She'd been spotted at the local OB/GYN's office, taking a then-pregnant Shannon for a checkup. Everyone in town had assumed it was Kate who was pregnant, not Shannon, a girl Kate had met while volunteering with the Big Brothers Big Sisters organization.

So Kathie could understand why Joe was reluctant to be seen in the place, especially in another meeting destined to make the gossip rounds.

"We have to," Kathie said. "And try to look happy when you see me. You're supposed to be crazy about me, remember? Otherwise, you can't be devastated when I break your heart in a month or so."

Joe fought the urge to drum his fingers on his desk, a habit he'd given up two years ago as a New Year's Eve resolution, because it wasn't good for a man to show any outward sign of weakness. Or stress.

And drumming those fingers was something he did when he was stressed.

Right then, he could have drummed with baseball bats quite happily, and it wouldn't have given him half the relief he needed considering what was about to happen.

Yeah, baseball bats.

And he had a quarter-inch-thick layer of glass lining the top of his desk to protect the wood from scratches. The bat would have made confetti out of it in seconds, but he wouldn't have cared.

She was coming.

And he was supposed to look happy about it.

"Mr. Reed?" his secretary, Marta, said from the doorway to his office, an odd look on her face. "Is everything all right?"

Joe hadn't known she was standing there, hadn't had a clue, and she wasn't a woman who moved with any kind of stealth. She was rather large, and besides that, she wore three charm bracelets with about fifty charms that jingled every time she so much as breathed. It drove him crazy, had for years, but it meant he always knew where she was.

Until today.

"I'm fine," he lied. "Why?"

"You buzzed for me to come in," she said.

He opened his mouth to say that he certainly hadn't, but then looked down to find one of his non-drumming fingers perilously close to the button on the phone that he used to summon her.

Maybe he had buzzed her in, one little drum of the fingers before he forgot he'd given it up.

"Is there something I can get you?" she asked.

"No. I…uhhh…I'm going to lunch. In a few minutes." He wouldn't be able to choke down a bite, but he'd go and try to look happy about it and not like a man about to get his head chopped off or something.

He wondered if Kathie had briefed her brother, the cop, on the let's-date-Joe-for-the-summer plan and how Jax might react, whether Joe would get hauled off into the woods yet again and threatened with bodily harm or more moving violations. If Joe was smart—and he'd always prided himself on being a very smart man—he'd park his car and walk to work for the next month. It was only a few miles, and the weather was fine so far.

Yeah, he should walk, just in case, at least until it got too hot.

Because a smart man knew how to pick his battles and avoid the ones he couldn't win. He'd never win with Kathie's brother over anything to do with him and Kathie Cassidy.

"Did I forget to write down an appointment, Mr. Reed?" Marta asked.

"No. Made it myself. Just now."

"Oh. With whom?"

He frowned at her, not wanting to say, wanting to postpone just for a few more minutes that nice, sane, everything-is-getting-back-to-normal atmosphere he'd tried so hard to cultivate after…the unfortunate event, as he'd taken to thinking of it in his own mind.

The series of unfortunate events, he should say.

She'd ended up in his arms more than once, after all.

He could have pleaded temporary insanity if it had been only the one brief time the day her mother died. Granted it had felt like temporary insanity each time, but he really couldn't claim a series of unfortunate lapses into temporary insanity. One didn't have serial bouts of temporary insanity. One had to consider it was more than temporary insanity at that point. More of a long-term psychological disorder, which he certainly hoped he did not have.

There'd been the day her mother died. Grief could have easily accounted for him taking her in his arms that day. Not for the kissing part, but the holding at least.

But the second time, the did-that-really-happen, Oh-my-God-it-did time, as he tended to think of it. The no-denying-it-anymore-time, trouble-is-definitely-here, what-the-hell-had-he-done-time. After which, he'd wallowed in guilt and confusion and, if he was really honest with himself, an overwhelming sort of…desire.

For his fiancée's little sister.

Rot in hell, Joe. You deserve it.

"Uhh hmmm."

Standing in front of him, Marta cleared her throat pointedly, then frowned at him.

"Sorry," he said. "Where were we?"

"Your lunch appointment? You were going to tell me who it's with, so I know to send him in when he arrives."

Joe tugged at his tie, which was getting tighter with every passing second. When had it gotten so hot in here? They'd turned on the air-conditioning last week, hadn't they? It wouldn't go off until sometime in September, at least.

He was starting to sweat when he realized something was going on in the bank. Or rather, that, oddly, nothing was going on in the bank.

A hush had come over the place. Through the glassed-in walls to his office, he could see that people had frozen in place and started to stare, mouths hanging open.

He leaned to the left, then the right, not able to see much of anything to either side of Marta. Her bracelet jingled, as she turned around, too, and started trying to figure out what was going on.

To the back of the lobby near the doors, he saw heads turning. More and more heads. She was halfway through the room now, judging by the stares.

Joe saw someone reach for a cell phone and hit speed-dial. Someone else looked like they were trying to ready their phone to take a photograph.

Great.

They could capture the moment for posterity and share it with the whole town.

When Joe met Kathie again, right there in the bank…

Marta gasped and jingled as her hand went, too late, to cover her mouth. "It's her!"

His secretary was fiercely loyal to him. She was one of the few people in town who didn't blame Joe for what happened. He noted with amazement that she had positioned herself between Joe and the door to his office, as if to shield him with her body from the walking disaster in the lobby, which had Joe fighting not to laugh.

The idea that Marta was so terrified of what might happen next to poor Joe that she'd physically stand between him and Kathie Cassidy was both sad and hilarious. Sad that she thought he needed protecting that much and hilarious at the idea that anything as insubstantial as a person standing between them would be enough to keep Kathie from doing whatever it was that she did to him.

Because he just wasn't himself around her.

It was like she short-circuited something in his supremely logical, well-organized, methodical brain, and he became someone he didn't even know, someone he couldn't begin to understand.

And what was his role in this charade today?

To act smitten?

He fought down another laugh.

Smitten?

Had he ever come close to being smitten with anyone?

Everything he'd ever felt for her sister had been completely reasonable and sensible. He'd been so happy to find someone who suited him so perfectly, who believed in the same things he did and had the same kind of calm, reasoned approach to life that he did. Theirs had been the completely rational, confident kind of courtship he'd always been seeking and feared he'd never find, because most women were…well, not so calm or rational or well-organized.

And Kathie…he would have never believed she was capable of causing havoc in anyone's life.

She could be quiet as a mouse most of the time. Kate was the one in charge, the strong, smart, determined one. Kim was the baby of the family, full of energy and exuberance. Jax was…well, Jax. As flashy and outgoing as Joe was serious and calm.

Kathie could easily disappear in the midst of them, hardly uttering a word. Sometimes when the whole Cassidy family was together, he forgot she was even there.

He'd known about the crush, of course. No way he could not have known. But that had been over for years, he'd believed. She'd always been kind to him, always noticed him but never done anything in recent years to make him think her feelings for him were anything but a history likely to embarrass her.

In a lot of ways, he'd still thought of her as a teenager. It was like she hadn't aged a day since he'd first met her, when Kate had brought him home to meet her family for the first time.

Little Kathie Cassidy.

His undoing.

"What do you want me to do?" Marta whispered to him urgently? "Get rid of her?"

"No, I don't want you to get rid of her," he said, all but prying open his own mouth after that and trying to force out the words, *She's my date*. No luck. He just couldn't get them out.

"I will if you want me to. I can do it. I get rid of people you don't want to see all the time. I'm good at it."

She made it sound like she'd been taking lessons from Jax, twisting arms and threatening people with broken kneecaps or something. It was a bank, for God's sake.

"No one's getting rid of anyone," Joe said. "She's here to see me."

"Not if you don't want her to. No one gets in to see you if you don't want them to."

"Marta—"

"I'm his lunch date," Kathie announced to what seemed like the entire building.

Marta gasped.

Maybe the entire room did, as well. Joe couldn't be sure.

He was too busy staring at her.

No naughty, French-maid-like outfit today.

Just jeans that were the tiniest bit snug and a little no-nothing, T-shirt-like top. Nothing that should have made her look so good, so young and fit and…

Something had happened to her while she'd been gone, he decided.

She looked…different. Not so teenage-girlish.

Oh, she still looked impossibly young to his thirty-one years, but not the way she used to.

Or maybe he'd just never really looked at her that closely because he'd never thought of her as anything but his fiancée's little sister. Until she'd kissed him that day, and then he'd simply tried not to think of her at all. Guilt had left him all but blind. He wouldn't even look at her, but now….

She looked different.

She looked…really good.

God, help him, he was headed straight for ruin again.

She was Kate only minus three years and a wealth of knowledge of how the world worked. Kate minus all the determination and drive and seriousness. Kathie was more carefree, a kinder, gentler, happier version of her sister, and he hated the whole idea of comparing the two of them. It brought to mind what a vile thing he'd done, being engaged to the one and kissing the other.

But as she stood before him that day, he couldn't help but think she was different in ways he didn't want to examine.

And that he was once again on the edge of sheer ruin because of the odd things he felt for her.

Kathie walked right up to him, stopping only a breath away.

Uh-oh.

Joe braced himself as best he could for what might come next.

Just how friendly were they going to pretend to be?

She put one hand against his chest, another on his shoulder, stood on tiptoes and kissed his cheek. While she was that close, she whispered in his ear, "You look like you're afraid I'm going to pull out a gun and rob the place, Joe."

Which was probably true.

He forced himself to try to relax, to let his hands rest lightly on her shoulders and smile as he brushed his lips against the side of her cheek, something he'd probably done a thousand times when he'd been engaged to her sister and never had so much as a remotely sexual thought.

Nothing but a friendly hello once again.

He could do this.

Except they were trying to look like more than friends, and she'd lingered too close, as did he, for a moment too long.

It only took a moment with her, her hand pressed against his chest, right over his heart, his face against hers, lips lingering beside the soft skin of her cheek, then his nose caught in the vicinity of her right ear, in the edges of her hair, taking in the smell of her.

He remembered this smell, so delicate, barely there. A man had to get this close to smell it.

Maybe it was the scent of her that did it, that went in through his nose and made a beeline to some part of his brain that just…couldn't take it, had no defenses against that sweet, intoxicating smell.

Maybe this was some weird, purely chemical reaction. Some imbalance in his brain. Twenty years from now, science would be able to explain, but for now, all he knew was that something in her did something to him and then…zip. It was like all the normal brain waves in Joe's head simply stopped. He was paralyzed, and all he could do was feel and smell and if he got a little closer, have a taste of her.

His hand came up to her cheek, and he dipped his head down low, finding the corner of her mouth, which fell open in surprise.

Just a taste, he told himself.

Just one, after all this time.

It was not a moment to hesitate. After all, if this craziness between them was still there, he had to know about it. Better now than later, so he knew what he was facing and could try to formulate some plan to protect himself and to keep from hurting her, enraging her entire family and the town once again.

That was right.

He had to kiss her.

His mouth found hers, his hand sliding to the back of her neck to tilt her head up ever so slightly to his. Her hands had a death grip on the lapels of his suit, and she was off balance now and leaning into him, her entire body brushing up against his.

He barely touched his lips to hers.

Barely.

Breathed in the scent and the taste of her, felt her quickly indrawn breath and her body start to tremble, felt the instant she started trying to pull away, to protect herself from this and from him and anything she might still feel for him, he feared.

Kathie, don't feel that way about me. Please. Not anymore.

But she did.

Oh, God, she did.

And she still short-circuited his brain.

What was he supposed to do about that?

He broke off the kiss and stepped back, his hands lingering on her shoulders to steady her for a long moment, her startled gaze locking on his, mad or hurt, he couldn't be sure.

And then, it was gone. She smiled up at him, like nothing had happened except a friendly greeting between people who were supposedly more than friends, a show put on for the noontime crowd at the bank, the beginnings of their whole charade.

What had he gotten himself into?

"Ready to go?" he asked.

She nodded, fake smile back in force.

"Marta, we'll be an hour or so," Joe said.

"Marta," Kathie said. "Sorry I...well, I was just so happy to see Joe, I forgot my manners for a moment. How are you?"

"Fine," Marta said, not sounding fine at all, sounding like she'd slipped into some alternate universe or something, where her boss had lost his mind again.

Maybe he had.

"Can we bring you anything from the diner?" Kathie asked.

"No. No, thank you. I brought a sandwich from home."

"Well, I guess I'll be seeing you around," Kathie said.

Great.

She took Joe by the hand, and he let her lead him out of the bank.

Chapter Four

Kathie got him out of there as fast as her legs could go without flat-out running. She kept a smile plastered on her face and her mouth clamped shut, when all she really wanted to do was scream.

At him.

At the world.

At her family for being here and being hers and making her want so much to be here, too.

But mostly at him!

Why did she have to care so much about him? Had years of misery over wanting him and not being able to have him—had all that not taught her anything? Months of guilt on top of misery, because she'd finally done something about wanting him, months of knowing her family knew and everyone in town knew what she'd done. Had those things not taught her anything?

Apparently not.

Because all he had to do was kiss her, and she wanted the damned man all over again!

And here she was, dragging him through the streets of downtown, about to embark on a make-believe courtship with him, all to keep everyone here from hating him!

She might have dragged him all the way to the diner and back, just like that, if he hadn't grabbed her himself, his arm around her waist from behind, actually lifting her up off her feet, and ducked into the alley beside the bank with him.

"What are you doing?" she yelled, drawing even more curious looks from people on the street.

He deposited her with her back against the bank wall, him up in her face and looking furious. "What am I doing? What are you doing?"

"Trying not to scream at you!"

"Kathie, you are most definitely screaming at me right now," he yelled back.

Oh, damn. She was.

She took a breath, then another, then sagged against the wall, grateful for its support. He had a hand on the wall beside her head, leaning into it himself, his other hand on his hip, as he shut his eyes and tried to calm down himself.

And he was still too close.

"Why did you do that back there?" she asked, unable to protect herself at all from this man anymore, unable to keep the hurt from her voice.

"Do what?"

"You know what. You kissed me."

"You kissed me first," he said.

"Not like you did, and you know it. Are you trying to hurt me even more than I've already let myself be hurt by you?"

"God, no. I would never do that," he claimed.

"Then why?"

"I don't know why."

She wasn't going to accept that. She was going to yell at him some more and make him tell her the truth, because no reason she could come up with made sense to her, and he was a very logical man. He had to know why he'd done it.

But then she looked at him, really looked at him, and something had changed in him. He didn't look logical or reasonable at all. He looked…baffled and frustrated and mad at himself.

His breathing wasn't at all steady, and she remembered something, remembered having her hand pressed against his chest over his heart, and how fast it had been beating back there in the bank.

She remembered the sweetness of his touch, the tenderness, the way he'd focused so intently on her mouth and sucked in a breath with his nose against her cheek.

The man was a lot of things, but an actor wasn't one of them.

He didn't play around. There was no subterfuge in him.

So what had he been doing when he'd kissed her?

One idea kept shoving its way to the forefront of her brain. That he'd done it because he'd wanted to.

Could he really want to kiss her?

"I don't know what happened back there, and I'm sorry," he claimed. "You just…caught me off guard, that's all. I don't like lying, and even when I was a little kid, I was lousy at the whole make-believe thing."

"That, I can believe," she said.

Actually, it was hard to imagine him as a little kid at all. Sometimes, she thought the man must have been born in a suit and tie and had worn one ever since.

And she was scared now.

Really, really scared.

Because that kiss felt like it had come from a man who just might want her, too. Could he possibly want her?

Kathie's heart started thundering. It was like all the breath went out of her body at once, and her head started to spin at the possibility.

Her legs turned to jelly, and she must have started to collapse onto the street, because he caught her hard to hold her up, ended up pressing her against the wall with his own body to keep her there, an expression on his face that she could not begin to read.

"What is it? What's wrong?" he asked, sounding genuinely concerned for her.

"Nothing." She went to push him away again when it was the last thing in the world she wanted to do, because she'd never been this close to him. "I was just...light-headed for a moment. It's gone now."

"Are you sure?"

She nodded.

He still hadn't let her go.

She was surrounded by him, chest, shoulders, arms, chin, mouth. There were muscles under that suit he was born in, in his arms and shoulders, his chest, and there was heat. He didn't look like a guy who'd have those kinds of muscles under his nice suit, or who'd generate that kind of heat. He'd almost always looked like a perfectly reasonable, pleasant, ordinary guy, just better. He'd always looked special to her.

But she felt the muscles now, felt the heat.

He smelled of fine wool and spice, clean and strong, and it was like everything in her had a way of responding to everything in him.

She wondered what he would have done if she'd taken his head in her hands and brought his mouth down to hers once more. If he'd have kissed her for real, and what that would have done to him, what he'd have looked like afterward.

She could plead light-headedness afterward and maybe get away with it.

Instead, her own cowardice won out, and she let her head fall to his shoulder, just for a moment and cling to him, like a woman exhausted and about to fall down without him to hold her up.

It wasn't far from the truth, and it bought her another moment here with him to try to figure this out.

Maybe he did want her.

It wasn't the silly crush she'd always had on him, and it certainly wasn't love. But it was something.

Something they could build on?

Something that might turn into love?

She shuddered, thinking of impossibilities and complications and how much hurt she'd already brought to so many people with this obsession she had with him. Just the possibility that he might feel something for her terrified her and excited her, both at the same time.

"Do you need a doctor?" he asked.

"Probably," she muttered to herself.

But he actually heard her and sounded worried. "An ambulance?"

"No, Joe." She laughed from sheer terror. "I just need a minute to…just give me a minute."

His arms came around her in an honest, tender embrace. He was worried about her. She could tell. She'd probably scared him, too. Not as much as the idea of him actually desiring her scared her, but scared him nonetheless.

Carefully, slowly, she eased away, standing on her own two feet and trying not to look him in the eye, not to show him any more than she already had.

"Sorry. I'm okay. Really." She glanced up and saw that he clearly didn't believe her. "I didn't eat anything last night, and then I didn't have anything this morning, either—"

"Kathie?"

"It was…things just got a little crazy. You know that. It was a crazy day." The first of many, she feared. "Let's go eat."

"Do you need me to carry you?" he offered.

"No. I'll be fine."

But he did put an arm around her waist and kept her close. She fought the urge to snuggle as they walked down the street, eyes following them everywhere.

What in the world had she done to herself by coming back here? By bringing herself back to him?

Their entrance into the diner had heads turning so fast Kathie was surprised no one got whiplash.

Mouths gaped open. As it had in the bank, all conversation ceased for a long moment, then picked up again in a furious rash of whispers.

The owner, Darlene Hodges, greeted them herself, no doubt happy about enhancing her restaurant's reputation as *the* place to be for anyone who wanted to know everything about everyone in town. Even better as a place to witness developments firsthand.

"Well, what have we here?" Darlene grinned, menus in hand. "Kathie, honey, it's about time you came home."

Kathie felt herself shrinking back from the whole scene, but that only put her in even closer contact with Joe, who stood his ground and kept her firmly planted against his side, probably still thinking she might collapse at any moment.

Perfect.

Just perfect for their little act.

"You two want a table or a booth?"

"Either one's fine," Joe said.

"Okay. Right this way," she said, leading to a spot smack-dab center of the room. Had to give everyone a good view.

It was a tiny booth for two. When they sat down, their knees bumped. They spent an awkward moment trying to get situated to where neither one of them was touching the other. The only thing they could come up with was an arrangement where Joe's knees ended up on either side of Kathie's.

"There we go. Sorry, it's a bit cozy," Darlene said, obviously not sorry at all. She handed them menus. "Special's chicken salad on toast today. Someone'll be right with you two."

Oh, this was bad, Kathie decided. So bad.

"I guess it would be even worse if we got up and ran out the door without having lunch, huh?"

"Definitely," Joe said.

Kathie fumbled with her little rolled up napkin and silverware combination, trying to unroll it and ending up with her spoon getting away from her and clattering onto the table.

More heads turned.

"Dammit."

She reached for it, because it was rocking back and forth making even more noise, and she wanted it to stop. Joe reached, too. His hand covered hers, and he held on to it, a million apologies in his dark brown eyes. But there was a steadiness there, too, something that said she could count on him, that he'd get her through this if she'd just let him.

How he could be so generous with her, when everything that had happened had so clearly been her fault, she didn't understand. He'd felt sorry for her, when she'd thrown herself at him the day her mother died, hadn't he? She'd surprised him? Horrified him? Just caught him completely off guard, and he'd reacted in a way any man might when a woman threw herself at him?

And then he'd realized what they were doing and backed off immediately, a look of complete disbelief on his face.

If only she'd left it alone then, maybe nothing else would have ever happened and no one would ever have known.

Everything would have been normal.

She wouldn't feel like a horrible sister, a horrible person, ashamed and full of what she could only describe now as a sick kind of longing for him. It was her guiltiest secret, that she'd wanted him the whole time he'd been her sister's. She'd also loved her sister dearly and was convinced her sister loved him. Which meant somebody had to get their heart broken. She'd always thought it would be her, not her and him.

Because she knew he loved Kate. She'd seen them together for years, knew them both so well, knew they were so well suited for each other.

Which meant she'd screwed things up completely for poor Joe.

Which was what she was here to fix.

Their waitress, Bree Hanover, who'd gone to kindergarten with Kim, showed up at their table positively beaming and shooting furtive glances at their still-clasped hands.

"Well, look who's back," she said, pen and pad in hand.

Kathie went to pull her hand away from Joe's, but

he would have none of that. He held on tight and smiled up at Bree, playing the role they'd agreed upon.

Fine.

Kathie would smile, too, even if it just about killed her.

They ordered quickly, sweet tea and the chicken salad special. Bree lingered, no doubt hoping for some choice bits of gossip, but they both just sat there holding hands and smiling up at her until she finally left.

From then on, it was one person after another stopping by their table to say hello. There were smiles and waves and outright stares. Mrs. Brooks from the library even offered Kathie a temporary job. Was it Kathie's imagination, or was the diner filling up completely? Soon there was a line at the door of people waiting to be seated.

Great.

They'd accomplished what they'd set out to do.

By nightfall, everyone would know she was back, that she'd been seen holding hands with Joe at the diner, that it looked like they were together.

Darlene came back to their table to see if they wanted dessert, which they refused, and then she turned to Kathie.

"Honey, I know this isn't what you normally do for a living, but if you need a job until school starts again, I'm short a waitress right now. Josie

Lawrence ran off three days ago with some hippie guitar player she met on the Internet, and we don't think she's coming back."

Kathie's mouth fell open. Work here? On display for the whole town? No way. "Oh, I couldn't. I mean I appreciate it, really, I do, but—"

"Mrs. Brooks at the library already got to her first," Joe said, saving her. "Annabeth Jacobs is starting her maternity leave next week. They need someone to fill in."

"Oh, that's right. She'll be out for most of the summer," Kathie remembered. Not that she wanted to work at the public library, either. Way too public for her.

"Well," Darlene said, smiling, no doubt thinking of the possibility of having record crowds at the diner all summer if there were any real developments on the Kathie-and-Joe scene. "If you change your mind, you know where we are."

Joe paid the check. They got to their feet and were nearly out the door when Charlotte Simms, the director of the local Big Brothers Big Sisters' program, spotted them.

"Kathie Cassidy," she exclaimed. "I heard you were back in town. Kate must be thrilled!"

Heads really turned at that one. Seemed everyone wanted to know if Kate truly was thrilled to have her sister back.

Kathie plastered on that smile once again. "Hello,

Charlotte." Then turned ever so awkwardly to Joe. "You know Joe Reed, from the bank, don't you?"

Charlotte's mouth fell open, the look of pure astonishment on her face almost comical. Obviously, she couldn't have been more surprised if Kathie had been having lunch with the Prince of Wales, right here in the Magnolia Falls' Corner Diner.

"Oh…of course…Joe. I've heard so much about you," Charlotte said, realizing what she'd just said and blushing furiously.

If the floor would have been willing to open up and swallow Kathie whole in that moment, she would have welcomed it.

"Nice to finally meet you," Joe said, the epitome of good manners.

Charlotte turned back to Kathie. "So, you're back? For good?"

"I…well…maybe—"

"We're all trying to persuade her to make it permanent," Joe said, rescuing her again. His hand settled at the small of her back, and she leaned into him, grateful for the support.

"And didn't Kate tell me you're a teacher?" Charlotte asked, digging into her purse and whipping out a business card. "That's perfect. I could use someone like you."

"Oh, I'm not really looking for a job. Not yet," Kathie said.

"That's good, because I don't have the money to

pay anyone." Charlotte beamed up at her. "So many of my kids at Big Brothers Big Sisters are behind in school, and they just need a little extra help to catch up. We've been hoping to start a tutoring program for them for the summer, and I need someone to organize it. I need a teacher. Which makes this just perfect."

"Well, as I said, I'm not sure yet if I'm even staying—"

"Just think about it," Charlotte said. "Come see me, and we'll talk, okay? You'll love it there. The kids are great. I know your sister really loved her time volunteering with us, and she got a husband out of the deal. I mean, is this a great place or what?"

Charlotte was still beaming up at them when it hit her that, once again, perhaps she'd said something she shouldn't. Still, Charlotte didn't let little glitches like that get her down for long. "It's all right now, isn't it? Water under the bridge and all?"

Kathie and Joe nodded, maybe not convincingly, but they nodded.

"Great. Joe, now that I think about it, I could use some help with money, too." She pulled out another card and handed it to him. "Maybe you could come see me? Or I'll come to you at the bank. Whatever works best for you."

"Sure," Joe said.

"No hard feelings?"

About Joe losing a fiancée to a guy she met at

Charlotte's organization? Kathie clamped a hand over her mouth to keep from laughing out loud. It was suddenly just too ridiculous to be standing here in the middle of the diner, everyone staring, talking about some of the worst days of her life. And for someone to say, *No hard feelings?* Like Joe had been cut off in traffic or something?

An alarmingly hysterical-like giggle escaped her.

"Not at all," Joe claimed, holding on to Kathie more tightly. "Nice to meet you."

"You, too, finally," Charlotte called after them as Joe hustled Kathie out the door and onto the street, where she started laughing like a mad woman.

Honestly, she just couldn't hold it back any longer.

It was crazy.

Her life was crazy.

"Okay, now you're scaring me," Joe said, dragging her into yet another alley, putting another wall at her back to help hold her up.

"Can you believe that?" Kathie asked, still laughing. "Oops, lost the love of your life to a guy she met at my office. Sorry. But I could really use your help with our finances! I mean…geez. Kate said the woman knew how to get what she needed, but this is ridiculous!"

Kathie laughed until tears started to leak out of her eyes and roll down her cheeks. Laughter and tears, all at the same time.

Oh, God. What an awful day. What an awful year.

"Kathie, come on," Joe said, hanging on to her until she slowly got control of herself, tears dried, laughter gone, leaving her feeling exhausted and so very sad.

"I'm starting to see what I left you to face all these months." One more thing for her to feel guilty about.

He shrugged, as if it had been nothing. "All we need is one good scandal in town, and we'll be old news."

She nodded. "I hope so."

He took her hand, tucked it into the crook of his elbow and walked her home. She saw a few window blinds pushed aside, furtive glances from a few of her neighbors as they walked past, and wondered if it would ever end, feeling impossibly weary and overwhelmed.

They stood looking at each other on the front porch. Kathie didn't think she had it in her to give him a friendly peck on the cheek again and was both relieved and dismayed when he did it for her.

Warm, soft lips pressed against her face. She got just a whiff of his aftershave and a sensation of heat from his body, and then he whispered goodbye and was gone.

She could breathe again.

This make-believe romance was going to kill her.

Chapter Five

Joe walked back into the bank, and it could have been last fall all over again. Heads turned. Furious whispering commenced and likely wouldn't stop for a solid week.

He hated this. Absolutely hated it.

Even worse was the way she made him feel.

She made him crazy.

That was the only word for it.

Crazy.

He was a man who'd always known exactly what he wanted in life, and crazy wasn't it. She wasn't it. Her sister was. Her sister had been everything he'd always believed he wanted, and how it had all gone so wrong, he still didn't know.

He made it through the lobby and to Marta's desk, which sat right outside his office. She looked like she was about to bust with all the questions she wanted to ask him about this most unsettling development in his life.

He held up a hand to silence her before she could even speak. "I know. I have a conference call in ten minutes. The file's on my desk?"

She nodded and held out a stack of pink slips. "You have sixteen phone messages."

He winced, taking them and not looking at one, made it into his office and said, "Later," then closed the door.

He sat down at his desk, would have leaned over it and buried his head in his hands if his office hadn't had glassed-in interior walls, which meant he could see practically everything that happened in the bank and everyone in it could see him.

One glance told him they were all still staring, dammit.

He picked up a file at random, opened it and pretended to be doing what he needed to do.

Three minutes later, Marta buzzed him. "You didn't say whether I should hold your calls, and... well, it's Kate Cassidy on line two. Or Kate... What's her last name now?"

"Taylor," he said.

"Kate Taylor. Want me to get rid of her?"

"No. I'll talk to her." Getting rid of them did no

good. The whole Cassidy clan, whom he'd once been sure was going to become his big, loud, happy extended family, didn't seem to be willing to let go of him and let him get on with his life. They were like glue, stuck to him, and he just couldn't get away.

He picked up the phone, punched line two, took a breath and forced himself to sound calm, not awkward, not upset, not anything at all he hoped. Neutral. That was it. All he had to be was neutral, leaning a little toward polite. He could manage that, he thought.

"Kate. Hi. What can I do for you?"

"Hi, Joe. I just wanted to thank you for bringing Kathie back to us."

Okay. That sounded genuine. It didn't sound like a stay-the-hell-away-from-my-sister-you-scumbag message, which he was sure would be coming from at least one member of the Cassidy clan. He'd go with the idea that Kate was genuinely thankful.

"She belongs here with all of you," he said. "I never wanted her to go away."

"Me, either. And I know I don't have the right to ask this of you, but…"

Oh, geez. What now?

Trying to be the gentleman he'd always hoped to be, he said, "What do you need, Kate?"

"I'm afraid she's going to leave again."

Joe did bury his head in one hand then, glassed-in walls or no glassed-in walls. "Already?"

"Maybe."

And was this after their little lunch date or before it, he wondered? Had he blown a simple lunch date so badly that she already felt like she had to leave?

I didn't do anything this time, he wanted to yell. *I didn't. I swear.*

"What do you want me to do, Kate?"

"Help us convince her to stay," she said.

"How?" He'd already fumbled the task of getting her to come back here. It was a complete disaster as far as he was concerned.

"I don't know. I just can't stand the idea of losing her again."

"Kate, I'll do anything I can, honestly. I owe her that. I owe all of you that. But I'm afraid I'm just going to make things worse. There doesn't seem to be anything I can do around her that's right. Somehow, it all comes out wrong."

And he'd never in his life faced any situation that was so frustrating. He always knew the right thing to do, and ninety-nine percent of the time, he managed to do it.

She was that awful one percent that completely defeated him.

Chemical imbalance? Or chemical reaction, he thought again? It had to be some weird chemical thing. The brain was a big jumble of chemicals, right? Thoughts, feelings, ideas, actions…all ruled by those pesky chemicals. She just threw his off, that was all.

"I have trouble saying and doing the right thing around her, too," Kate said. "I just wanted to ask you to try. Maybe we can drag out this whole summer plan of hers—"

"She told you about that?"

"Yes. Last night."

"Look, it wasn't my idea. It just kind of came out in conversation, and it was the only thing I said the whole time at that fancy boarding school of hers that she listened to. I thought it was my only chance to get her back here. That's the only reason I went along with it."

"I figured it must have been something like that."

"So…you're okay with this? With Kathie and I seeing each other for the summer?"

"Yes, just… Be careful, Joe. Don't hurt her."

"I never wanted to hurt her. I swear to you."

"I never thought you did. And I don't have any hard feelings about any of that. I promise. When I asked you not to hurt her, I just meant…well, I'm afraid it would be so easy for you to hurt her again."

Oh, hell.

"Because you think she still…has feelings for me?"

Kate was silent for a long time. "Maybe."

Which was the same thing he'd feared when

he'd kissed her and held her and felt like he couldn't have added two and two together if his life depended upon it.

"That makes no sense at all," he protested

To which, Kate laughed. She'd laughed more in the last six months than she had in the entire time they'd been engaged, Joe thought. Maybe that was where he'd lost her. He'd never made her laugh.

"It doesn't," he protested. "You know it. Kathie and I, even when nothing happened…. I mean, God, Kate, hardly anything ever happened, I swear, but it tore her world apart, and that's the last thing I ever wanted, to hurt either one of you."

"Joe, if this was about logic, you and I would still be together," she said. "But we're not talking about logic. We're talking about feelings."

"I'm so much better at logic," he complained.

And Kate laughed again, even harder than before. "I know, but you'll figure this out. I have complete faith in you and your ability to figure things out."

"And I don't have any. Not in this," he admitted, wishing so hard they could just go back in time. All he needed was a little more than a year. He'd still be engaged to Kate, still understand everything, still have a plan for her and him.

They'd go back to right before her mother died, to spring of the previous year. He'd have never taken her sister in his arms to try to comfort her that heartbreaking day, never kissed her, never torn his carefully composed life apart. He'd know what he wanted, and how he was going to get it. He wouldn't have ever been this confused or crazy. Life would have gone on, just as he'd expected it to.

"Look," Joe told her, "just so you know, in case it helps you with her, Kathie doesn't seem to believe that you've forgiven her. Or that you're truly happy with your husband."

Truth be told, Joe felt the same way. Was she truly happy with her new husband? It wasn't his ego talking…at least, he didn't think it was. He just couldn't imagine Kate changing her mind so completely and so quickly. One minute they'd been engaged, and the next she'd married Ben, a mere three months after she met him. They'd gotten engaged after only six weeks, and that was something Joe would never have believed Kate Cassidy would ever do. She was too much like Joe, and it was certainly something Joe would never do.

"I was afraid Kathie thought something like that," Kate said. "I keep trying to tell her I'm happy, but it doesn't seem to do any good. It's like I'm telling her the sky is the color of grape jam or something, if she'll even let me bring up the subject. Maybe by the end of the summer, she'll see for herself. When you got her to agree to come back, it was only for the summer, wasn't it?"

"That's what she said. I know it's not what you all want, but it was all I could do to get her back at all."

"I understand. It's going to take all of us to keep her here."

It would, and if Joe understood his part in it correctly, he was supposed to be seen with her, act like he liked her, but not too much, because she might still have a thing for him. He wasn't supposed to hurt her, but he was supposed to help her want to stay? It was impossible, just like the mess he'd faced last year, once she'd kissed him and he'd kissed her back.

Good God, if only someone would tell him what to do.

He glanced up to find Marta going nuts, trying to get his attention, pointing to her watch and then holding up the phone. His conference call was coming in.

"Kate, I'm sorry. I have to go. I'll do my best. I'm not sure if that's going to be good enough, but I'll try," he said, then looking up to signal Marta that he was getting off the phone, not to freak out on him.

But Marta wasn't paying any attention to him. She was staring into the bank, as she had been earlier that day when Kathie came in.

Everyone, he noted, was staring again.

Surely not Kathie, not so soon.

He wasn't up to it.

He needed some time to prepare.

He stood up and tried to see, heard shouting, a man's voice this time.

Kate was still talking, thanking him again, something he knew he didn't deserve. And then, the half dozen customers in the bank shifted in just the right way, and Joe saw what they all saw.

Jax, charging toward him, a look of complete disgust on his face.

Oh, dammit. Not again.

"Kate?" he said, interrupting her. "You said you heard about Kathie's plan, this thing where we pretend to see each other for the summer plan?"

"Yes."

"Do you know if your brother's heard anything about it?"

"I don't think so."

"Maybe one of you could tell him," Joe said, as Marta, a full foot shorter than Jax, bravely used her short, rounded body to try to block the door to Joe's office.

"Jax won't like it," Kate said.

"I know," Joe agreed.

He would hate the plan.

The only question was, what would Jax hate more? The idea of the keep-everyone-in-town-from-hating-Joe, even-if-they-blamed-Kathie-instead plan? Or the idea that Joe and Kathie might be seeing each other for real?

Again, no way to win, as Joe saw it.

"Okay, I'll tell him," Kate said. "Or I'll have Kathie tell him. I'm not sure which would be better."

"Are you absolutely friggin' nuts or something?" Jax yelled over Marta's head, as Marta bravely stood her ground in the doorway.

"Either one would be better than me having to tell him," Joe told Kate. "Which I'm about to have to do. Right now."

"You mean—"

"Yeah, he's here, and he's not happy."

Joe put down the phone and fought the urge to straighten his tie, something he always tried to do when some kind of trouble showed up at the bank. Like a straightened tie would ever help him with anything like Kathie's brother, furious at him— again.

"I mean, you've got to be a flaming idiot. That's the only thing I can figure out," Jax yelled.

Marta looked over her shoulder and said, "Do you want me to call security?"

"He's a cop, Marta. Our security guy's a retired cop with thirty-five years on the force. If it came down to me or Jax, I think Jax would win and I'd hate to make Harry have to choose," Joe said. "Just let him in and close the door."

She did so reluctantly and very, very slowly, positively glaring at Jax. Just before she closed the door, she added, "I go to church with your boss. You'd do well to remember that before you come in here and make trouble."

Joe nearly laughed. Marta went to church with just about everybody. It was like she considered the congregation her own private hit squad. Anybody caused trouble, she expected one of her fellow church friends to take care of it for her.

"You think this is funny?" Jax roared, the walls positively rattling at the sound.

"No," Joe said, disgusted.

The phone at Jax's side rang. He grabbed it, looked at the number of the incoming call and then frowned.

Come on, Joe thought. *Pick it up.* Kate could handle him so much better than anyone, except maybe Jax's fiancé, Gwen.

No such luck. Jax shoved the phone into his pocket and let it ring.

Great.

"Want to tell me about your day, Joe?" he asked, glaring at him as he leaned over Joe's desk.

"Not particularly," Joe said, fighting the urge not to lean back in his chair to get away from him.

"How about lunch? Want to tell me about lunch?"

"You already know. Kathie and I had lunch."

Jax's phone rang once again. He swore softly and then started pressing buttons on the phone. Joe thought he was answering the call, but no. He did something to it and then shoved the phone in Joe's face.

"There. That doesn't look like lunch to me. That looks like you dragging my sister into the alley behind the bank and kissing her!"

And…yeah, that's what it looked like. Not the dragging part. The kissing part. Someone had snapped a picture, with a camera phone it seemed, of him kissing Kathie at lunch.

"I had five of these damned things beamed over to me by three different people. You and her here at the bank, kissing. You and her at the diner holding hands, and best of all, you and her in the alley."

Joe shook his head, trying not to groan. This was small-town living at its best, coupled with a wave of cutting-edge technology. Nothing like it. He should move to Atlanta, even if he did despise the traffic. No one would know him there.

"You know I could kill you and just make up the reason why and get away with it, right?" Jax yelled.

Joe nodded. He believed it. "But Kathie wouldn't like it. And neither would Kate."

Which only made Jax madder.

"What do you want me to do?" Joe yelled right back. "Lie down and die right here? Believe me, I've considered it. I've done every damned thing I know to make this better, and none of it's worked. You told me to get her back here. I didn't want to. Hell, it was the last thing I wanted to do. But you wanted her back, so I got her to come back, and now that I did—"

Behind Jax, someone gasped.

Marta, he realized. Marta, guarding the door again with her four-foot-eleven-inch body, and behind her...

Oh, hell.

Behind her and just to the left, nothing but half her face visible, stood Kathie, pale as could be and looking like she wished she could sink into the floor and die.

Jax turned around and swore.

He really would kill Joe now.

Kathie was here.

She'd obviously heard every word, and Joe had just made everything infinitely worse.

They all stood there—frozen—for the longest moment.

Marta, probably for the first time since she'd come to work for Joe, looked at him with absolute disgust. She was the first one to move. She took poor Kathie by both arms and went to steer her away from the disaster zone.

"Honey, let's you and I go right over here," Marta said.

"No. Thank you, but I think I'm done here,"

Kathie said, still pale as could be, staring from Joe to her brother and back again.

It was much the same look she'd had on her face the first time she saw Joe after their whole sordid secret had come out. Stricken, stunned, embarrassed, like she was in agony, but still on her feet somehow.

"Kathie, wait," he said, heading around his desk and to her.

"No," Jax said, shoving a hand against Joe's chest hard to stop him. "You've done more than enough."

But Joe shoved right back. He wasn't going to let Kathie leave this way. "Kathie, I swear, I didn't mean it that way. You have to let me explain—"

"Explain what?" She shook her head, turned and ran.

"Kathie!" Jax yelled at her.

Marta again blocked the door, defending her from both of them now.

"Let me handle this," Jax yelled.

"No," Joe yelled. "I am done listening to you!"

It turned into a shoving, shouting match to get to the door, with both of them tripping over Joe's chair and a plant until, still hanging on to each other, they landed hard against one of those glass walls of Joe's office.

It rattled ominously, but held.

They glared at each other some more.

"You're dead," Jax said, loosening his grip on Joe only long enough to draw back his arm, ball his fist and slam it into the side of Joe's face.

Joe felt the punch connect. Damn, that hurt. Felt it propel his whole body, already off balance, against the glass wall once again, the momentum of the punch hurtling Jax forward as well.

Then, he heard another crack.

An odd tinkling, then a rumble, and they both went hurtling through the glass and onto the floor of Marta's office.

People screamed.

Bits of glass fell like rain, showering them as they lay in a stunned mass on the floor beside each other.

Joe felt something stinging at the corner of his eye. His jaw was numb. The arm he was lying on felt like someone was poking him with little nails, and he wanted to get off them, but wasn't sure if moving in the least was a good idea because there was glass everywhere.

"Oh, my God!" Marta gasped.

Someone yelled for someone to call an ambulance.

Someone else yelled to call the cops.

Jax groaned at that one.

Joe put a hand to the side of his face, and it came back bloody. He could feel it now, blood rolling down his face. He went to roll off the glass under his arm, but ended up landing on even more glass, and then his back hurt as well.

"Don't move!" Marta yelled. "You'll only make it worse. Not that the two of you don't deserve it. That poor girl!"

"Is she gone?" Jax asked.

"Oh, yes. She's gone."

"You've got to call Kate," Joe said. Kate was their only chance. "Tell Kate what happened—"

"I'm sure half the town is calling Kate right now to tell her what just happened. I'm ashamed of both of you. Brawling in the bank like teenagers!"

"Listen," Jax said. "You have to call Kate to tell her to find Kathie and stop her from leaving. Not yet. Not until I get to talk to her—"

"I have to talk to her," Joe yelled.

"Just call Kate," Jax yelled. "She's probably the only one who could keep Kathie here." He tried to move himself, then gasped and went still.

They both lay on the floor, glaring at each other, glass all over them both and on the carpet between them.

Joe had never been in a fight in his life.

That he'd chosen to now, at the ripe old age of thirty-one and in his place of business in front of a dozen customers and employees—all over a woman—was unbelievable to him.

"I'm gonna rip your damned head off," Jax said.

"Oh, shut up!" Marta said.

It looked like she kicked him in the shins, she was so mad.

They lay there in silence after that, first hearing sirens, then a commotion behind them. The firemen, in full firefighting gear, showed up first, giving them both the oddest looks. One of them belonged to Joe's church. Another's wife worked at the bank, and they all seemed to know Jax.

"Should we try to get 'em out first, or get the paramedics in here to look over them?" one of the firemen asked.

Another one shrugged. "Anybody having any trouble breathing?"

"Nope," Jax said.

"No."

"Doesn't look like they're bleeding too badly," the second fireman said, the glass crunching under his heavy boots as he waded into the midst of the mess, running his hands quickly over Joe's extremities, and then Jax's. "Think either of you broke anything?"

"No, I just have glass under me," Joe said.

"My wrist feels funny, but that's it," Jax said.

Joe felt about a million stitches coming on. He wondered how they'd get the blood stains out of the rugs, and how in the world he'd ever be able to explain this to his supervisors. They'd think he'd literally gone nuts, and that might be the only thing that kept them from firing him outright.

"Let's get backboards, just in case," the fireman

from Joe's church said. "No reason to haul 'em out by their arms and legs if we don't have to. Call dispatch. Tell 'em one ambulance is enough, if you two can be trusted in one together?"

Joe closed his eyes and groaned. Jax made more of a growling sound.

Marta was still lecturing them both, and one glance told Joe the crowd in the lobby of the bank was growing every moment.

He laughed then. He'd been sure things couldn't possibly get any worse.

And he'd been completely wrong once again.

Chapter Six

They were carried on backboards out of the bank and into a waiting ambulance for the five-block trip to the hospital.

It seemed fully half the town's population had gathered outside to see what was happening. There was speculation about bank robbers, Jax just happening to be in there, and he and Joe fighting off the robbery attempt.

If only that were the case.

Joe lay there, miserable, embarrassed and worried about Kathie. The emergency medical service guys had cut off his jacket and his shirt. He'd kept his pants, over their protests. They'd pressed a pad of gauze to the side of his face near the corner of his right eye and bandaged a gash in his leg where there was one particularly deep cut.

He was considering asking them for some kind of painkillers, maybe enough to knock him out. Maybe when he came to, he'd see that this was all a nightmare.

The idea that he could have ever done anything like this was about as remote as Joe joining a nudist colony or taking up smoking crack as a pastime. It just didn't compute with anything he'd ever imagined.

Jax had landed funny on his arm or wrist and maybe broken one or the other. Joe hoped it hurt like hell. He wished the guy had broken his mouth, and they'd have to wire it shut, so Joe wouldn't have to listen to anything the guy said for at least six weeks. Too bad he didn't think people could break something like a mouth. Maybe his jaw, although knowing Jax he'd still find a way to give Joe hell, jaw wired shut or not.

Of course, Joe hadn't even hit him, so there was little possibility of Jax having a broken jaw.

Maybe Jax had broken Joe's jaw, and it would have to be wired shut, so Joe wouldn't have to talk to anyone for weeks.

Yeah. That didn't sound bad.

They were loaded into the ambulance, the paramedic in the back having no doubt heard the whole sordid story because he was grinning like crazy.

"Kate's going to have a fit," he told them both with maddening glee.

Joe squinted out of his good eye and eased to the right, so he could see the kid. He knew Kate?

"She did the mortgage on mine and my wife's house, did my parents' house, too. My mom's Shelly Andrews. Used to teach at the middle school when Kate was there. And I used to date Kate's secretary before I met my wife. You guys have had some year, huh?"

Joe just closed his eyes and prayed for a long-lasting sedative to spare him from some of what was to come.

They rolled up to the emergency room not five minutes later, where more people than necessary seemed to be milling around the waiting room as they were wheeled in.

"This is really not necessary," Jax argued.

"You let us be the judge of that," a pretty nurse at Jax's side said.

Joe thought Jax used to date her in high school. Jax had dated everybody.

He and Jax found themselves parked in side-by-side cubicles, worked over by at least a half dozen people each, all looking exceedingly curious as the two were examined once again.

Joe eventually found himself lying on his stomach while a doctor dug bits of glass out of his back and arm. Someone else put fifteen stitches in his left leg just below his knee. An ophthalmologist was called in to look at his eye, which was finally pronounced free of glass or punctures, the area around it bruised from the punch he took and messed up from a cut that took another eight stitches to close.

"You're going to have a nice shiner from this," the doctor told him.

Someone took Jax off to X-ray his arm, but it turned out he'd done nothing more than sprain his wrist. He had a few minor cuts and was getting stitched up at the same time Joe was, when Jax's fiancée, Gwen, came rushing to his side.

She looked horrified, had obviously been crying and could hardly speak.

"Gwen, I'm fine. Really," he said, while the doctor stuck a needle into his head.

She gasped, finally got out, "Someone tried to rob the bank?"

Jax turned to Joe and glared. "Not exactly."

Gwen looked over at Joe and whimpered once again. "I heard someone tried to rob the bank. That you were right in the middle of it."

"He was in the middle of it, all right," Joe said.

The nurse standing nearby laughed.

Gwen took Jax's hand in hers, looking worried and confused. "There was no robber?"

"No, honey. No robber."

"Then what happened?"

"Just a little misunderstanding," Joe said.

"An accident," Jax claimed.

At which, poor Gwen looked even more confused. "But…people said you had blood all over you, and that they took you away in an ambulance, and that they heard a shot."

"Not a shot. Just a big piece of glass that shattered and cut us up a little bit, and did this." He held up his newly splinted wrist. "Just a sprain. I landed funny. That's all. I promise."

She looked a little less panicky. "I was so scared."

"I know, honey. I'm sorry. I was hoping I'd be able to call and tell you before you heard it from anyone else, but…well, I'm sorry. Things have been hectic and…Gwen, it may be better if I met you at your house later."

"Why?"

"Joe and I have some things we have to take care of," Jax said.

"Like getting their stories straight," the nurse said with a grin.

"Stories?"

"Gwen—"

"What happened?" she asked, looking from Jax to Joe and back again.

It was like Joe could see the possibilities running through her head, none of them good.

"Wait a minute. Did someone e-mail you a

certain photo supposedly taken today at the bank or maybe at a certain restaurant at lunch?" she guessed.

"Try five," Jax said, all hope of finessing his way out of this—at least with his fiancée—obviously gone.

"You two got into a fight? At the bank?"

"We had a discussion," Joe tried.

"And then…a little accident, right? It was an accident," Jax claimed.

"Yeah. An accident," Joe agreed.

"He tripped and fell, took me down with him. Through one of those big glass walls in his office at the bank," Jax claimed with the kind of aplomb Joe couldn't help but admire. He'd never been a good liar. But if he was ever going to be one, now would be the time.

Gwen came closer to Joe, staring at his bruised cheek. "And the wall did that to the side of your face?"

Joe shrugged his shoulders. It was possible. He didn't know what had been caused by the punch and what had been done when he hit the glass or landed on the floor. He didn't know what the side of his face looked like.

Gwen went back to Jax and grabbed his right hand, none too gently despite the splint, to inspect it. "And I guess the wall bruised your knuckles, too? Because you went through it fist first."

Okay, they were busted.

Gwen turned and walked away.

"Gwen, come on," Jax yelled. "I'm sorry. I am."

"I don't know you," she called out, without even turning around.

"Wait. Can you find Kathie? Has anybody seen Kathie this afternoon?"

That got her to turn around. "She saw the two of you fighting?"

"No. Just…heard him say some things he shouldn't have," Jax said, back to glaring at Joe.

"While you just stood there like a choir boy?" Gwen suggested. "Waiting for a chance to throw him through a wall?"

"I didn't throw him through anything. He tripped."

She turned and walked away again, not stopping this time.

"Well, that went well," Joe said.

Jax's boss showed up next, one very unhappy man in search of an explanation. Joe would likely be hearing from his own boss, who'd likely be just as unhappy about a bank president getting into a brawl over a woman in the middle of his bank. Brawling with a cop just made it even more interesting.

They stuck to their story of falling, an accident, in the midst of nothing but a discussion. Jax's boss clearly didn't believe it, but he left without arresting anybody, which they took as a good sign. Although Jax had been ordered into the man's office first thing in the morning.

It was still far from the worst either man would face.

Kate would let them both have it, and be perfectly justified in doing so. But Kathie would be hurt and embarrassed and likely find a way to blame herself for the whole thing.

Joe felt like a complete jerk.

"I need a phone," he told the nurse, because he had no idea where his was. Probably somewhere on the floor at the bank in the suit they'd cut off of him. "I have to call someone."

"She's my sister. I'll talk to her," Jax said.

"You two are going to fight about who gets to call her now?" Kate appeared from around the corner, fuming. "Great. That's great. Because it's not like either one of you has done enough yet to make this whole thing even worse!"

She stopped for a minute to consult with the nurse. "Are they okay?"

"Sprained wrist on this one, maybe fifty stitches between the two of them. They were lucky it was safety glass. It's designed not to tear open an artery when people smash through it."

"Do you think we could get this one's mouth stitched closed?" she asked, pointing to Jax.

"Hon, if we offered that service, we'd make a

fortune. We'd have people lined up around the block begging us to do that to all their relatives."

She nodded, understanding, then moved on to Joe. "And you? I can see him doing something like this, but not you. Joe, what's gotten into you?"

Her whole family, he thought. Her entire family.

He'd been absolutely sane and perfectly reasonable until he'd met them. He was discounting completely the fact that he'd been sane as could be for the first four and a half years he'd spent engaged to Kate. It was only the last year that had turned him into a man he didn't even recognize.

"Kate, I'm sorry," he said.

"After I asked you to be careful with her?"

"To be careful with her?" Jax yelled. "What do you mean, be careful with her? We don't want him to be careful. We don't want him anywhere near her!"

"No, what we don't want," Kate said, "is for you to be anywhere near him, Jax. You are not helping."

She fumed silently, then looked completely overwhelmed. Poor Kate had hardly ever been overwhelmed in her life.

"Did you find Kathie?" he asked, when she got done bawling them out.

"She and Kim are probably right behind me, although all they want to know is whether you'll both live. Beyond that, we're all ready to disown both of you, and by all of us, I mean Gwen, too."

Kim and Kathie arrived three minutes later.

They stood side-by-side, arm-in-arm like they needed to hold each other up, staying a good ten feet from the end of the gurneys that held Joe and Jax. It was obvious that they'd both been crying, both been worried, but at least Kathie hadn't taken off and left town yet.

She looked them both over quickly, then turned to Kate.

"They're both okay?"

Kate nodded.

"No robber? No shots fired?"

"No," Kate said.

"It was what we thought?"

Kate nodded.

"Okay." Kathie turned to Kim. "Told you so."

Kathie looked at them both once again, her expression a cross between annoyance and a terrible kind of hurt, then turned and started to leave.

"No!" Kim yelled, grabbing her and refusing to let go. She started to cry, big tears rolling down her cheeks, and she looked about sixteen again, even though she had just turned twenty-one. She grabbed Kate's hand and dragged them both to the end of Jax's bed. "This is all that's left of our family, the only one we've got. We cannot tear it apart. I won't let that happen. I need you all too much. Not just one or two of you. I need all three of you, so we're just going to have to find a way to get along. All of us."

"Kimmie," Jax began. "I'm sorry."

"I don't care if you're sorry. Sorry doesn't cut it anymore. It's time to work it out," she said, then turned to Kathie. "And you. I know they're both jerks, but you are my sister, and you said you'd stay until the end of the summer. You promised. No matter what."

Kathie still looked like she was ready to cut and run. Jax had talked about having someone run by her house and steal her spark plugs or something, until she'd calmed down. Joe hated to admit it, but it didn't sound like a bad idea.

She couldn't go like this.

"Kathie, I didn't mean it," Joe said. "Not like that."

She silenced him with a single look.

"Tell us what to do," he tried instead. "We'll do anything you say, if you'll just stay."

"You don't want me here. Remember? That part came through loud and clear."

"I told you, I didn't mean it—"

"Yes, Joe. You did."

"I'll be the one to go," he said. "It's your town, not mine."

"I don't want anybody to leave," Kathie said. "I just don't want anybody fighting, and I'd really like it if no one ever talked about me or my life ever again, including my entire family. I'm through pretending. I'm through trying to change anyone's mind about anything. I just want everybody to leave me alone."

"Okay," Joe said.

It would be nice to leave her alone, wouldn't it? Then he wouldn't hurt her anymore, and he wouldn't have to try to make things better for her.

Normally, he could fix anything, but not this.

He could just give up.

Walk away.

The relief should be overwhelming. So why did he feel so lousy all of a sudden?

"What about me?" Jax asked.

"I may never talk to you again," Kathie proclaimed, turning and leaving.

Kim glared at them both, her gaze finally settling on Jax. "Me, either," she said, then turned and followed her sister out.

Kate waited until they were both out of earshot, then came closer, examining the little cuts and bruises on the side of her brother's face, looked down at his fingers curling around the end of his splint, touching them lightly. She turned to Joe, frowning over his eye with the eight stitches in the corner of it and the big gauze pad around his leg.

"You both look ridiculous, and you're going to look even more ridiculous tomorrow with all the swelling and bruising you'll have by then," she told them. "Now that I know there wasn't more bloodshed, I'd like to smack you both, but that would just give the town something else to talk about."

"Kate—" Jax tried.

"No. I don't want to hear it. If either of you care about Kathie or this family at all, you'll take a vow of complete silence to each other on anything to do with Kathie. I mean it. Not a peep. And don't bother trying to explain. We know exactly what happened, and just in case it wasn't clear earlier, we blame you both."

And then one more woman turned and walked out on them.

Kathie didn't cry anymore on the way home.

She was done crying.

She was, however, considering standing outside, fist raised in the air, a defiant look on her face à la Scarlett O'Hara, where she swore she'd never go hungry again. Except Kathie would swear never again to care what Joe or her brother thought, what anyone said about her and maybe not about anyone else's feelings. Except her baby sister when Kim had insisted they hold their family together. That was right, and Kathie did need them all, even Jax when he wasn't in overprotective, older brother mode.

Kathie thought about her vow, liking it.

If she really didn't care what anyone else thought, there was no reason to leave. Everyone would just have to get used to what she'd done and get over it.

She was done hiding, done apologizing and done feeling lousy about the whole mess.

Later that evening, Joe was lying on his sofa, holding an ice pack against his swollen face, feeling ridiculous and embarrassed and mad when his doorbell rang.

"Go away," he called out.

He heard a key in the lock. Had he ever bothered to get the key Kate had to his house back? He didn't think so. So it was either Kate or his mother, who had a key because she was sure there would be some caretaking he'd need that only she could provide if she had a key. He really had to get that key away from her.

With effort, he raised up off the cushions far enough to look over the back of the couch and see his mother standing in the open doorway, a look of utter dismay on her face.

"Go away? That's how you greet people who show up at your door? With, go away?"

"Sorry, Mom. Bad day." He eased back onto the cushions, his head pillowed by one end of the couch.

His mother stood over him, frowning and bewildered-looking. "Were you raised in a barn? With the manners of a goat? Because that's what people would think when you spout off things like, Go away!"

Joe sighed and covered his face with the ice pack.

"It's that girl again, isn't it? The wild one."

Which actually made him laugh, even if it did hurt his side and his face.

"She is not wild. There is nothing wild about her. In fact, there's not a wild one in the whole trio of Cassidy sisters. Their brother, on the other hand, is a complete barbarian."

"Who has you brawling in the middle of your bank? I couldn't believe it when I heard. I'll have you know that every single one of the women in my bridge club called me to tell me about this. My son, in a brawl, in his place of business? Did they fire you yet?"

"Not yet."

She sent up a whispered plea for divine intervention, then said, "The girl is obviously nothing but trouble."

"She's not. She's just…her family's a little intense."

"You never had trouble with the family before, when you were with Kate. Her family was fine then. It must be this girl," she said, helping herself to a seat opposite him. "Tell me you're done with her."

"She is done with me," he said. She'd probably never speak to him again.

"Good. Maybe now things can get back to normal. There's a wonderful young woman whose mother just joined the bridge club. She's as practical and responsible as can be, quiet, careful, and always, always, always on time. I know how important that is to you. She's a woman who would never cause you a bit of trouble, I'm sure. Why don't you let me introduce the two of you?"

"I do not want another woman. I don't want any woman," he said. "I'm thinking of becoming a monk."

"But she's perfect for you."

Truth was, she sounded like the perfect appliance repairperson, given the emphasis on punctuality. But not at all like a woman he'd want to date.

"I mean, I know she's not Kate, but—"

Joe fought off a groan.

His mother loved Kate. Adored her. Thought she was the perfect woman. Definitely the perfect wife. He feared that his mother still believed Kate would come to her senses one day, leave her new husband and come back to Joe.

If only it were true. He imagined his whole life, magically returning to normal, that all of this would be an aberration. A mirage, maybe. He didn't care if they weren't in the desert, and he wasn't dying of thirst. Couldn't this whole thing be a mirage?

He moved his jaw to the right, testing it.

Still hurt.

A lot.

Okay, maybe it wasn't a mirage.

"Mom, I think maybe it's time for us to give up on the idea of Kate and me. It's just not going to happen."

"Nonsense. People change their minds all the time and walk away from perfectly adequate marriages. We know that," she said, a thinly veiled reference to her own husband, who'd walked out on them when Joe was eight.

Truth be told, he'd walked out many, many times when one or another of his financial schemes collapsed or over some woman. But the time when Joe was eight had been the worst, and it had stuck. He'd been having an affair with the woman who lived across the street. She kicked her husband out, and Joe's father moved in, right across the street from Joe and his mom.

Until his father pulled one of those deals he kept pulling, some start-up business that went belly-up after a few years or an investment scheme that wasn't quite on the up-and-up, and his father was broke again. The neighbor woman kicked him out, then lost her house to boot, having put it up as collateral for his father's latest business. They both ended up moving away, and then at least, Joe and his mother didn't have to see them every day.

"Kate's not going to leave her husband. I don't want her to leave her husband," Joe said, trying out the idea and seeing how it felt. He didn't want her to come back to him. He couldn't. Her sister was still making him crazy, and he needed to get over every single one of the Cassidys. The only one who'd never caused him a bit of trouble was Kim, the baby, and he didn't want to take any chances that her turn might be coming. "Mom, I just want…"

"What, dear? What do you want? How about dinner with that nice young woman I was telling you about?"

"No. No dinners. No nice, young, punctual women."

"Okay. No dinners. Drinks?" she tried.

"No!"

"There's no reason to shout. I know you're upset, but I'm your mother!"

"Sorry. I'm sorry. Really."

"It's just that awful girl. It must be. You've never behaved this way before. You've never talked to me this way."

"Mother, there is nothing awful about her. She's a perfectly nice young woman. You know that. You've met her, and you liked her just fine until last year."

"That was before she did those things to you and ruined everything."

"It wasn't like she attacked me," Joe said, because his mother simply couldn't face the fact that Joe would ever do anything wrong. He'd appreciated it when he was eleven and fifteen and nineteen, but at thirty-one, it was getting ridiculous. "And it wasn't like she forced herself on me."

As if Kathie would have ever done that.

Sure, she'd surprised him. Shocked him, in fact. But shocked or not, he'd wanted to kiss her, and he had, more than once.

"Joseph Daniel Reed—"

"Mother, I love you, but don't do that," he insisted.

No one could have been more shocked than she'd been at the unexpected turn his life had taken, and he was sorry about that. But she'd developed a bossy streak that was becoming unbearable. She'd taken to lecturing him, using all three of his names, and trying to order him around again, like she'd done when he was a kid.

And the whole thing was his fault. The whole situation had sad echoes of his father's behavior over the years. People had loved to talk about his father. He and his mother had lived with it their whole lives. So it was no surprise that Joe had lived most of his life trying to be as responsible and respectable as could be, never causing anyone any trouble.

Until a year ago when Kathie Cassidy had thrown herself into his arms.

"Just be done with this woman," his mother said.

"I am done with that woman," he agreed.

"Thank God. Now everything can get back to normal."

Joe shook his head. The thing was, he feared his life had taken an irrevocable turn, and there was no going back.

"It'll be all right," his mother said. "You're a good boy."

Joe fought the urge not to bang his head against the wall, and reminded himself that as the only son of a long husbandless, aging mother, he had a special responsibility to look out for her. And it wasn't all responsibility. He did love her, very much, and it had been just the two of them for so long.

He just couldn't have her blaming Kathie the way she wanted to.

"Think about my friend's daughter," she said. "Maybe I'll have her drop by the bank one day this week, just to say hello."

"No. No one else is coming to the bank about anything except bank business."

Hell, he didn't even know if he'd still be there.

He finally got his mother out the door, laid back down on his couch with his ice pack and tried to work up his nerve to apologize to Kathie somehow for what he'd said.

He started calling her apartment at eight-thirty. Called every half hour until ten-thirty and then realized she was either not there—and had maybe packed her bags and left despite Kim's plea—or she was just not going to pick up the phone.

Fine. He'd tell the stupid answering machine.

It would probably be better if he didn't actually have to talk to her, anyway.

He called again and let the machine pick up.

"Kathie," he said, "Just don't erase this without listening to it, okay? You don't have to say anything back. Not ever. But let me say my part. I do want you to be here. I want that because this is where you belong. This is your town. It's your family, and I know how important they are to you, and how important you are to them. They were all pitiful without you. I don't think they can stand to be here without you, but most of all, I don't want you to be without them. I know how much you love them. I know how much you depend on them."

He paused, took a breath, then rushed on, afraid the tape would stop.

"Kathie, I would never forgive myself if you stayed away because of me. That's why I came to find you and get you to come back. Not because your brother threatened to beat me up. Because this is where you belong, and I was worried about you when you were gone. We all were. And I owed it to you to make sure you came back because—and I know you don't believe this, no matter how many times I've tried to say it—I was as much to blame for everything that happened as you were. More, actually. I was the one who was engaged. I was the one who was supposed to be in love, and I'm thirty-one years old. Certainly old enough to know my own mind and control my own actions.

"I know you loved your mother very much, and for me to have made things even harder for you in the middle of that… I just can't believe I did that. I've always tried to live my life a certain way, to not hurt other people, especially ones I care about, and I failed in that completely last year."

That was the part that really got to him. How completely he'd failed Kate, Kathie, their entire family, himself, his mother, all those people.

"Look, could we just be done with this? All the awkwardness and confusion and hurt feelings? It would be so nice to just be done with it all, to try to get back to normal. You're here, where you're supposed to be. Your family loves you. Jax, crazy as he can be, is only that way because he loves you and worries so much about you. If I had a little sister and someone had done this to her, I'd have punched the guy, too, and a lot sooner than he actually did."

Okay, maybe that wasn't a good idea, bringing up the whole brawl thing.

Did it actually count as a brawl? Because Joe had never been in one, and he really didn't know.

"Anyway, I'm sorry about earlier. Really, I am. I was just mad at Jax and at myself. He hasn't said anything about me that I haven't said to myself. I just hate hearing it from him. When I said I didn't want you back here, what I really meant was that I want things to get back to normal, and I was afraid if you came back, everything would get stirred up again."

That he might get confused again, do something really stupid again, and show that he did have the manners of a barn animal.

Which is exactly what had happened, with a speed that was truly alarming.

Not something to point out to her.

This was about making things right. Ending the guilt. Restoring order.

"I am truly sorry. Jax and I swore to Kate that we wouldn't say a word to each other about you from now on. We mean it. Kathie, I just want you to be okay. I want you to be happy, and I want you to do that here, where you belong. Please don't leave because of me or the stupid things I said."

He finally hung up the phone, not quite sure what he'd said, just that he thought he'd said it all.

Time to move on. He'd stay away from her brother, maybe go meet Miss Punctuality who'd so impressed his mother, and then…

Joe had no idea.

His face hurt. His leg hurt. He had a horrible headache, was maybe unemployed and his mother was lecturing him like he was an adolescent again.

He groaned, closed his eyes and willed it all to go away.

Chapter Seven

Kathie listened to the message—in its entirety—as he left it, her sister sitting on the sofa beside her, silent and hopeful-looking.

"He sounds like he means it," Kim said, when it was finally over.

"I know."

"I mean, it's Joe. He'd never be mean enough to say he didn't want you here, even if he meant it. Not that I think he meant it," Kim rushed on. "It had to be Jax. You know he can make anybody crazy."

"I know," Kathie said, hugging a yellow throw pillow to her chest, legs drawn up beneath her as she leaned back into the corner of the sofa.

"You have to stay. You just have to."

"I said I would," she reminded Kim.

"We'll go hiking, and have a cookout at the lake or spend a weekend at the beach. We'll sleep late, and get great tans and not grade a single paper or make a single lesson plan all summer. How about that?"

"Okay," Kathie said.

She would have agreed to just about anything at the moment.

A trip to the beach. A trip around the world. A trip to Mars. All those sounded good.

Kim finally gave up on watching her as if she feared Kathie would escape the first moment she had alone and never come back, which didn't sound bad to Kathie. Finally her sister went to bed, and then Kathie did, too, not expecting to sleep. But she did, and the next thing she knew, it was morning.

Kim had cracked open Kathie's bedroom door and was peeking in, a worried look on her face.

"What's wrong now?" Kathie asked.

"I'm afraid Jax is here."

Kathie groaned.

"He doesn't seem mad. In fact, he's perfectly calm, and Gwen is with him. Gwen seems mad. At him. And Kate's here. They want to talk to you."

She frowned and looked at the clock. "It's not even eight."

"I know. They all have to get to work, and I think they were afraid to let this go until tonight. The only good part about the whole thing is that they brought a surprise for you."

Kathie was scared of any surprise her brother might spring on her, but then Kim opened the door further and a gorgeous, caramel-colored Australian shepherd came bounding into the room, barking excitedly. He put his front paws up on her bed and licked her face.

"Romeo, baby. Hi. I've missed you," she said.

He woofed in return, grinning like crazy.

A tiny white ball of fluff, prissy as could be, trotted in after him and leaped onto Kathie's bed, just as excited.

"Hello, Petunia. You are as pretty as ever, and I missed you, too," Kathie said.

Romeo had been her mother's dog, and hugging him was the closest Kathie could get to hugging her mother now. Her mother had loved Romeo so much. Jax had him now, and the love of Romeo's life, Petunia, belonged to Jax's fiancée, Gwen. Kathie wrapped her arms around both of them and let them kiss her face.

"You know, we could just hide out here in my bed and refuse to get up and see anyone," Kathie told the dogs. "We could cuddle up with each other and nap and just forget all about them. How about that?"

It would serve her brother right.

He was only trying to soften her up, by bringing the dogs this way.

Petunia wiggled her little tail and settled in next to Kathie. She was always up for a nap, and she loved sleeping on the bed.

Romeo was still grinning for all he was worth. He was the sweetest thing.

"Or we could wait for everybody to leave and then go to the park. Would you like that?"

Romeo woofed to show that he would, and Petunia would go anywhere he did.

It sounded much more pleasant than anything else Kathie could think of.

But Kim, still standing in the doorway, said, "You know they won't leave without seeing you."

"All right. Fine," she said, getting out of bed and pulling an old sweatshirt on over her pajamas. "We'll get rid of them, and then we'll go to the park," she told the dogs.

She didn't brush her teeth, or comb her hair or do anything else. If her family couldn't let her sleep after the disaster of a day she'd had yesterday, this is what they got when they came to find her.

She stalked defiantly into the living room, followed by the dogs, and stopped right in front of her brother, arms folded in front of her and waited, trying not to notice or care that he looked like he'd been in a barroom brawl.

The side of his face was a mess of little cuts, scrapes and bruises, worse than they'd been the day before. She didn't want to think about him going through a glass wall face first, even if it was his own fault. His right wrist was in a brace of some sort, he'd busted his lip at the corner and he was the closest thing to a father she'd ever known. She had hardly any memories at all of their father, who'd died when she was five.

When he didn't say anything right away, just stood there staring down at her with the saddest expression on his face, Gwen and Kate both elbowed him hard.

"Okay," he said. "Kathie…oh, baby, I'm—"

She couldn't help it, because as crazy as he made her, she loved him dearly and he'd spent his whole life looking out for her. She launched herself at him, into his arms, burying her face against his chest and feeling his big strong arms come around her, locking tight.

She fought back tears and demanded, "Not another word about me and Joe and that whole mess. Not one word."

"Not a one," he promised.

"Not ever."

"Okay. Never."

Kathie backed up and looked him in the eye. "And that means not a single word to Joe, either."

"Kate already made me promise not to ever speak to him about you again."

"And no fighting."

"Okay, I will not lay a hand on him, never again."

"No falling? No tripping?" she said, because her brother was sneaky. "No accidents of any kind in his presence?"

"None."

Kathie felt like this was a genuine opportunity that might never come along again, and she decided to take advantage of it.

"And not another word about any man I…one that I…" She sighed and just couldn't say it. It certainly hadn't been a love life that she'd had with Joe. Not any kind of life at all. And it hadn't been a relationship. What to call it? "Not another word about me and any man I choose to do anything with. Not ever."

He hesitated at that one. That would be harder.

Kathie backed away and stared at him, her sisters, Gwen and the dogs backing her up.

"Oh, okay," he said, throwing up his arms in surrender.

"And you can't try to convince my husband to do your dirty work for you," Kate announced. "You're through corrupting him."

"All right."

"And no more getting your friends on the police force to harass Joe, either," Gwen said, holding Petunia in her arms.

"What?" Kate said.

"You did what?" Kathie glared at him.

"Just a few moving violations, that's all."

"No more," Gwen said.

"All right. No more anything like that."

"And you can't turn all your attentions to me and anyone I choose to date, either," Kim added.

"Fine."

"You look awful," Kim said, leaning closer to inspect the side of his face. "And you scared me yesterday, you rat! You scared all of us."

"Sorry." Then he turned to Kathie. "So…you'll stay?"

"For now," she said. She wasn't promising any more.

And then they all looked pitiful again, even Romeo. He planted himself against her side, putting his head right beneath her hand, so she'd pet him, and looked up at her with big, sad eyes. He even made his silly crying sound, as if to say, *How could you leave me? Don't you miss me? Don't you love me anymore?* The guilt-inducing abilities of her family knew no bounds.

"Tell her the good news," Kate said to Gwen.

Gwen immediately perked up. "You have to stay, at least for the next month because Jax and I have given up waiting on my mother's broken hip to heal and for her to get up out of bed and come to the wedding. I mean…it's been three months. She won't go to physical therapy because she's still pouting because Jax and I plan to live here instead of in Virginia, where she is, and I guess she thought if she put it off long enough, we'd change our minds or something—"

"Or maybe that Jax would do something, and you'd change your mind about wanting to marry him," Kathie suggested.

"Hey," Jax yelled. "None of that. She loves me. She's crazy about me."

"She'd have to be," Kathie said, unable to stop herself from grinning at that. Her brother was one of a kind.

"And she's going to marry me a month from now," Jax announced.

"Ben had a couple cancel a wedding, so there's an opening on the calendar," Gwen explained, "and we figure your brother's bruises will be healed by then, so…we're going to do it."

"Good," Kathie said. "It's about time."

"Yes, it is," her brother said.

Kathie knew he'd been bending over backwards to try to win Gwen's mother's wholehearted approval for the marriage, even agreeing for months to postpone the wedding until she was fully recovered and could attend the ceremony. All because he knew how important it was to Gwen to have her mother there. But apparently, they were through putting off their own plans in an effort to placate the woman. Good for them.

"A month doesn't leave us much time," Gwen said. "Will you help us, Kathie? You and Kim?"

"Of course, we will," Kim said, looking eagerly at Kathie, waiting for her to agree.

"Sure. Just tell us what you need."

"Everything. We need everything."

"Come on." Kate grabbed Jax by the arm. "That's our cue to leave."

The town was abuzz for days about the big fight at the bank.

Kathie ignored it all as best she could, kept her head up and went about her business, helping Gwen with wedding plans.

She managed not to come face-to-face with either one until she literally bumped into her brother as he was coming out of the coffee shop early in the morning a week later.

He barely managed not to spill the tray of the four coffees he carried.

As usual, heads turned and curious eyes followed them every moment as Jax followed her back inside.

"You okay?" he asked.

She nodded. "Did your boss make up his mind yet? Did he suspend you?"

"I'm good. No suspension."

A cop in uniform slugging the bank president and sending him through a glass wall in his office in the middle of the business day did not pass without notice by his superiors. The way she'd heard it, he and Joe both covered for each other and swore the whole thing was an accident. Jax's boss hadn't questioned anyone else who might have proven their story wrong, something he certainly had a right to do.

It was probably only out of deference to their father, who'd been on the police force and died when Kathie was five while trying to stop a convenience story robbery, that Jax wasn't fired. That and the fact that most everyone loved Jax.

Still, Kathie had worried about him.

"I'm behaving very well," he told her.

She frowned at that. "Trying to score points with everyone at the office by bribing them with the best coffee in town?"

"Yeah." He grinned easily. "And stuck on desk duty for two weeks. The chief had to do something. No big deal."

Kathie would never mind him sitting behind a desk for any reason. She still worried about losing him the way they'd lost their father, but he'd never wanted to be anything but a cop and normally, there was no telling Jax anything.

"Thanks for helping Gwen with everything," he said.

"You're welcome."

"See you." He slid to the right, to get around her, but then the door opened, and there was Joe, limping slightly as he came inside.

Jax backed up to make room for Joe to enter. Kathie gasped. Maybe half a dozen other people in the shop did, too.

They were both still cut up and bruised from their now legendary battle with the glass wall and each other. People seemed to expect more bloodshed before they were through. But as Kathie watched in surprise and gratitude, Jax merely nodded at Joe, his mouth tightly shut, as if someone had stapled his lips together. Joe nodded in return.

"Very good," Kathie whispered to them both as they stood just inside the front door. "Could you both manage not to look so grim?"

Jax stiffened at that, but managed to coax the ends of his mouth up a tad. Joe did the same.

"Excellent. Jax didn't lose his job," Kathie told Joe. "Did you?"

"No, I didn't."

"Suspended?"

"The bank doesn't suspend people," he said.

"Put on probation?"

"Not exactly."

"What did they do to you, exactly?" Kathie asked.

"It was a cross between a threat and a warning, I guess."

"Lovely."

"No more than I deserved," Joe said, glancing carefully at her brother.

Joe seemed to be enjoying the fact that Jax couldn't say a word to him. Now that she thought about it, Kathie was, too.

"Jax was just leaving," she said, reaching out and opening the door for him, then practically shoving him through. "Bye, Jax."

He went through the door without a fight, but that was it. If he intended to stand on the other side of the coffee shop's door and stare at them, so be it.

Joe moved to put his own body between her and her brother, blocking Jax's view. Apparently they weren't past a case of one-upmanship toward the other.

"You listened to my message?" Joe asked.

Kathie nodded, easing closer to him to keep anyone from hearing what they had to say, then found herself simply too close.

"I really am sorry," Joe said.

"I know." Kathie kept her head down, her gaze firmly locked on a spot on his tie. She practically had her nose pressed against him. It was like she could feel the whole room closing in around them, like the whole place had just leaned closer and turned an ear toward them.

Joe moved to put his back between her and as much of the room as possible, then leaned down to whisper close to her ear. "I didn't mean it, I swear."

"I know."

She tried hard to ignore that little hitch in her

breath, the shiver that went through her as she felt his warm breath on her ear. Or maybe it was just the sound of his voice.

Oh, God, he still did this to her!

What would it take for her to be cured of this man?

He stood there awkwardly. "Are you coming in or leaving?"

"Coming in," she admitted.

"Come on. I'll buy you cup of tea. You still like the spicy stuff? What's it called?"

"Chai."

"Okay. Let's show everyone we can be civil. Let's sit down and have a drink together."

"Okay." Kathie wasn't about to admit that she couldn't so much as sit and have tea with him in a public place without falling apart.

If she was going to stay here, they had to come to some understanding. Hopefully he would never understand what it cost her to do things like this with him, until sometime when she didn't still feel this way. Maybe they'd laugh about it someday— this obsession she'd once had with him, the misery she'd felt at the idea of never being more to him than his ex-fiancé's little sister.

It could happen, right?

He ordered their drinks, and they found a table and sat.

Another tiny table, unfortunately.

Had someone shrunk all the tables in this town?

She sat in her little chair, as straight and tall as possible, ignoring the fact that her right knee was bumping against his left and that he sat maybe six inches away from her. The last people who'd sat here must have been a couple, a couple who'd wanted to be practically in each other's lap in the coffee shop.

Kathie folded her hands primly in front of her, dismayed to realize a moment later that she was twisting them together, this way and that, like a woman who just couldn't remain still. Joe, she noted curiously, was drumming his fingers on the table until he noticed that she'd noticed, then stopped.

"I'm…uhh…glad they didn't fire you," Kathie said. It was the first thing that came to her mind.

"Me, too," he said, not looking as grim as he might have, all things considered.

"I'm sorry about everything," she said.

"Me, too. Although I have to admit, it's been interesting walking around looking like I've been in a brawl. There was a woman on a Harley…a biker-woman in black leather pants, who gave me a serious once-over yesterday as I was coming out of the grocery store. I mean, that kind of woman would never have given me a second look without what's left of the black eye and the bruises. So, this is a whole new experience for me."

"Brawling Joe?" Kathie managed a genuine, she hoped not-heartbroken smile. "No, that is definitely not you."

"And Marta? It's like her whole job description has changed. You should see the way she's constantly scanning the front door of the bank, like she took a surveillance course from the CIA or something and is always on alert for trouble now. The bank will be more secure for decades because of this."

Kathie actually laughed then. Heads turned. She was determined to ignore it and try not to look like she just wanted to sink down into the floor.

"I think she's truly frightened by your family. Like she's just waiting for one of you to storm the bank at any moment. I tried to explain to her that you're an exceedingly peaceful person, and that most of your family is, too, but I can't get her to budge on her opinion of you all."

"Oh, well. I may have to move my bank account. Wouldn't want to traumatize your secretary unnecessarily."

"That's another thing," Joe claimed. "The activity level at the bank's gone up exponentially. People just keep trying to find a reason to hang out there, waiting to see what's going to happen next. If we can get just a fraction of these people to open an account or take out a loan, we'll have one of our best quarters ever. It's nothing I'd have ever put in a business plan, but it's proving to be highly effective."

The waitress brought Joe's coffee and Kathie's tea. Kathie wrapped her hands around the cup and inhaled the sweet, spicy aroma. It was so odd, having a drink with Joe, laughing over the brawl and Joe trying to tell her it had actually helped instead of hurt him.

He'd do that to try to make her feel better.

That's the kind of man he was.

"So, are the job offers still pouring in to you?" Joe asked.

She nodded.

"But you haven't accepted any of them?"

"Not yet, but—don't laugh, okay?"

"Okay."

"I'm going to take Charlotte Simms up on her offer to volunteer at Big Brothers Big Sisters."

"You're kidding?"

"No. It was a genuine offer, and she has a genuine need for help. I spent some time with Shannon, helping her practice her essay writing. She just took the SAT for the first time last month, and the new essay was giving her fits. It was nice to be able to help her."

"I'm sure it was," Joe agreed.

Kathie sat there and tried not to think of what might have happened if things had been different. If he hadn't come into their lives because of her sister. If Kathie had seen him first. If he'd fallen in love with her, not her sister.

It was simply too hard. It hadn't happened that way, and there was no changing it. Disaster averted was the best she could hope for, and that wasn't a given, not yet anyway.

"So," she said, going on with her story. "I went to talk to Charlotte, and she said when kids' lives fall apart and they end up in foster care, their education is usually one of the first casualties. They have to change schools many times. Their parents are gone. Their friends are gone, and they just don't care about anything for a while. A lot of them get behind and need some extra help. That's something I can do, something I think I'll actually enjoy. Plus, it's not like committing to a regular job for any length of time."

"Kathie—"

"I'm not saying I'm going to leave town." Or that maybe she wouldn't be able to stand to be in the same town with him, smiling and laughing and pretending her heart wasn't broken every time she ran into him. She wasn't saying that at all. "It's just that the volunteer thing with Charlotte keeps my options open."

He hesitated, looked like he wanted to say more, but settled for, "All right. If that's what you want to do right now, I can understand that."

Ask me to stay, Joe, she thought. *What would it*

take for you to ask me to stay? To want me to stay? To want me at all?

Of course, he didn't do that.

"Although," she said, looking for something to say until she could escape, "a friend of your mother's made a strong case for teaching abroad, English as a second language in Thailand, of all places."

Joe's mouth fell open. "You're kidding?"

"No. Someone from her bridge group. She said it would be a grand adventure for me, and that every young woman should have at least one grand adventure in her life."

"I'm going to strangle her," Joe practically yelled.

Kathie gave a start. Joe never yelled.

Even more people stared.

"What is it?" Kathie asked.

"My mother. She's getting to be as pushy as your brother."

"You think your mother put her friend up to trying to talk me into going halfway around the world?"

"Yes," Joe admitted, then looked immediately chagrined.

Kathie's smile disappeared. "So, your mother hates me now?"

"No. Not that."

"It must be something like that if she wants me in Thailand."

"She just worries."

"About you being on the same continent as me?"

"She might be taking that same CIA course as Marta," he said, no doubt trying to make Kathie smile.

It wasn't going to work. Not about this. "I always thought your mother liked me, that she liked all of us."

"She did. She just…it's a plan cooked up by her and one of her bridge pals. Or maybe the whole bridge group is talking about us and plotting. One of them has a daughter. I'm told she's fanatically punctual. My mother and her mother want us to date."

"Oh," Kathie said, taking a long, slow sip of her tea because she wanted to hide her face behind the cup.

Joe dating someone else?

She hadn't thought of that, although why she wouldn't have, she couldn't understand. Of course, he'd be dating other women eventually. She should have expected it, and it shouldn't hurt this much.

"Well…you've always thought punctuality was important," Kathie said.

Joe made a skeptical sound that was half laugh, half disgust. "Still, I'm thinking that the fact that she's punctual being the first thing anyone thinks to mention, doesn't bode well. And the fact that punctuality would be on top of my list of personality traits for a date…what does that say about me? Am I really that dull?"

"No. Not at all," Kathie argued. "You're so… solid. And dependable."

Maybe not qualities that would first spring to mind to most women when it came to whom they might want to date, but given the life Kathie had lived, incredibly appealing to her. She craved dependability like some people craved drugs. That was another thing that had been so bad about the previous year, that so many things had hit them out of the blue, so many things had changed. Kathie hated change.

Joe made a face. "You think I deserve Miss Punctuality."

"No. That's not it."

"I'm afraid I might. But I will speak to my mother about getting her friends to encourage you to leave town. I'll put an end to that today."

"No. It's okay—"

"It's not," he said, his hand reaching out to cover the one of hers that was lying on the table between them.

She tried not to think about it, her hand covered by his, tried not to feel anything at all. Especially about him and Miss Punctuality. Did she really have to stay here and watch him date other women?

Thailand didn't sound bad next to that.

His own mother was trying to get rid of her.

Mothers had never hated Kathie. They'd never tried to get rid of her. She'd always been such a good girl.

And she was trying to ignore it, but there was still that little spark of awareness between them. All he had to do was smile at her, and she felt it. It was even more evident when he did something as simple as hold her hand.

God help her, it was still there.

Joe squeezed her hand. Her eyes came back to meet his.

"I don't want you to go," he said, and looked guilty just saying it.

"But a part of you doesn't want me to stay, either."

"It's me," he said. "Not you. I just don't seem to be able to think things through the way I used to. It's like my head is a jumble and all the circuits just don't connect anymore. It's baffling. Like I said on the phone, I think I'm going through a phase."

Kathie cocked her head sideways and studied him in the way she might an exhibit under a microscope.

He couldn't think straight?

Joe?

He did look confused, now that she studied him more closely. And not happy about it.

He let go of her hand and pushed his empty coffee cup away, getting ready to leave, and she didn't want him to go.

Not yet.

It was starting to get really interesting here in the coffee shop with him.

"Everybody gets confused, Joe."

"Not me. Not until last year. My mother thinks I need therapy. My boss suggested it, too. Me? Therapy?"

Kathie laughed. He said it like it would be akin to eating bugs or something.

"A friend at the Lions Club suggested I try rock climbing, said it would give me a chance to clear my head. Can you imagine me needing to climb the side of a mountain to clear my head?"

She shook her head.

"I mean...I'm pretty sure I'm afraid of heights. So I guess I could go and think of nothing but how terrifying it was, hanging off the side of a mountain with nothing but a rope and a few spikes holding me up. But that isn't my idea of a helpful, head-clearing activity. It's got to be a phase. Midlife crisis, just early."

"Of course. You've always been an overachiever. I can see you hitting the midlife crisis ten or fifteen years early," she agreed.

"Well...if I don't leave now, I'm going to be late. Marta would be so shocked, she'd probably call the cops and report that I must have been kidnapped or something. I've never been late getting to the bank in my life, and that would just be one more rumor to fly around town right now."

"Don't need that," Kathie agreed.

"It was good talking like this," he said. "We can do this, Kathie. We can get everything back to normal, don't you think?"

"We can try."

"Good. I'll see you."

"Bye, Joe."

She sat there long after he was gone, trying not to look melancholy or hopeful or freaked out or anything like that.

He couldn't think straight?

Joe?

That part just didn't compute, not with anything she'd ever known about him. He was normally as logical, sensible and careful as Kate. It was one of the reasons everyone had always thought he and Kate were perfect for each other, because they were so alike.

But now he couldn't think, and that had to mean something, didn't it?

Most surprising of all to Kathie—who was trying hard not to even think of this—was that last fall, when Kate had first met Ben Taylor, a man she'd agreed to marry after a whirlwind, makeshift court-ship of only six weeks, Kate had said the same thing.

That she just couldn't think straight.

That she didn't know what was right anymore.

That nothing made sense to her.

Kate, who was as all-out logical as Joe had always been.

It's not you. It's not you. It's not you, Kathie told herself, trying to calm herself down.

She was not the one who'd done this to him.

Although, it certainly didn't sound like Miss Punctuality had done it.

Kathie wanted to scratch the woman's eyes out anyway. It was shocking, how jealous she felt of the woman, and she and Joe hadn't had so much as a first date.

But his mother wanted Kathie to go to Thailand, and for Joe to date Miss Punctuality, because she thought Kathie was the bad girl in this whole mess.

Not fair at all.

And not fair that she might get her hopes up again and then her feelings crushed in the end, when it turned out that Joe was just confused, not that Kathie had left him practically incoherent, unable to even think straight.

Oh, God.

Not again, she argued with herself.

Not one more time over this man.

Chapter Eight

With her brother's wedding moving ever closer, Kathie joined her sisters, Gwen and Shannon at the local dress shop the following week for power shopping. The dresses had been ordered months ago, before Gwen's mother broke her hip, but they had to do the final fittings, find shoes, plus find a dress for Shannon.

As they waited for her to model the latest dress they'd all insisted Shannon try on, Kate came to wait with Kathie, both of them still in their bridesmaids' gowns of pale yellow satin, Kathie still waiting for her turn with the alterations lady.

"Shannon looks so grown up, doesn't she?" Kate said.

Kathie slipped her arm around her sister, trying to be mindful of yards of yellow satin. "So much happier, you mean. She's like a brand new person. You did good."

"We're getting pamphlets in the mail from colleges already." Kate blinked back tears. "Her adoption isn't even final yet. We can't start thinking about giving her up to college already."

"Come on," Kathie said. "This family never really gives anyone up. Plus, I also know you'd never hold her back in any way, especially not from getting an education."

"That doesn't mean I can't be sad about it," Kate said.

Shannon came out of the dressing room in a pale blue dress with a billowy skirt. She was making a face that said she found it appalling.

"Okay. You were right," Kate said. "Definitely not you. Try the fitted one."

Shannon grumbled, picked up her billowy skirts to reveal a pair of black high-top sneakers underneath that had Kate cringing as Shannon headed back into the dressing room.

"I thought I'd burned those shoes," Kate called after her.

"No, they were in the back of your closet. I thought you'd borrowed them and just forgotten to give them back," Shannon said, laughing.

Kate rolled her eyes, then laughed herself. "What

can I say? It's not the most traditional mother-daughter relationship, but it works for us."

"I would have thought you'd done so much mothering of Kim and I that a teenage girl would be the last thing you wanted," Kathie said.

"Me, too." Kate shrugged. "You just never know what life will bring you."

The alterations lady, Miss Nancy they'd always called her, had a son who'd been one of Jax's closest friends since nursery school. She waved Kathie over to her little part of the store, in front of a three-way mirror.

Kathie dutifully went, the dress making a crinkling, rustling sound as she walked. It wasn't bad, as far as bridesmaids' dresses went, rather plain, which Kathie liked, with a scooped-out neckline that stretched out onto her shoulders. There were little cap sleeves, a fitted waist and billowy skirt.

Kate followed her, having already been pinned and tucked herself.

"You've lost weight," Miss Nancy said, frowning at Kathie, and pulling out her pins to mark places in the bodice where she'd take the dress in.

"Maybe a couple of pounds," Kathie admitted.

"'Bout time you came home. Your mother would not have tolerated you running away like that," Miss Nancy said.

"Yes, ma'am," Kathie said meekly.

"I'm going to need more pins. Don't move," the woman ordered.

Kate laughed when they were alone once again. "She always scared me."

"Me, too," Kathie said.

"Stuck me three times while she was taking in my dress. I think her eyesight's going."

"Now you tell me," Kathie complained, then glanced up into the mirror, seeing her reflection and Kate's, side-by-side, laughing as they so often did, marking another milestone by getting ready for their brother's wedding.

"If you cry, I'll cry, too, and I don't want to cry anymore," Kate said.

"I'm trying not to. It's just that we got so used to losing people in our family. I never thought that one day, we could start adding them instead. I like this. I love Gwen, and she seems to adore Jax and make him happy. I never thought about him giving us another sister by getting married, but I like it."

"Me, too," Kate said. "I want to do nothing but add to the family from now on."

Miss Nancy arrived with her pins, catching the last comment and glancing pointedly at Kate's waist. "If you need to tell me something, do it now. I know two weeks doesn't sound like much, but under certain situations in the dress alterations business, it can mean a lot of work at the last minute when you keep secrets from people like me."

"I have no secrets," Kate assured her. "The only person we're adding to our family anytime soon, other than Gwen, is the teenage girl in the dressing room."

"You're sure?" Miss Nancy asked, pins in hand.

"Positive."

She kept her eagle eyes on Kate's waist for another moment, like she didn't believe it for a minute, then finally turned back to Kathie, spinning her around to work on the back of the gown.

Kate made a frightened face, now that Miss Nancy couldn't see, and they both giggled.

"I wasn't going to talk about this yet...it's so new, but we might be adding to the family in other ways," Kate said.

Kathie, puzzled, didn't get it. "You mean, Gwen is pregnant?"

"Ahhh!" Miss Nancy shrieked and stuck Kathie with a pin at the same time.

"Ouch!" Kathie said.

"Hey, what's going on over there?" Kim asked from the other side of the shop, coming up from the foggy euphoria of shoe shopping just long enough to notice the uproar.

"Nothing," Kate called out, then, more softly, said, "No. That's not what I meant."

Miss Nancy glowered at them. "Do not frighten me like that. Especially when I have sharp objects in my hand."

"Sorry," Kate said.

"Do you have any idea what's involved in altering a wedding gown for the kind of expanding waistline—"

"There are no expanding waistlines in this wedding. I swear," Kate said.

Miss Nancy finally calmed down and went back to work on Kathie's dress.

"I was talking about Ben and I, and what we might do once Shannon's gone," Kate whispered. "We were talking the other night, and he said if we miss her too much, we can adopt a whole houseful of teenagers, if we want."

"Kate!"

"I know. I thought he was crazy when he first said it, but who knows? You and Kim were teenagers when Mom first got sick, and I feel like I understand teenagers. I look at Shannon now, and I think, 'Okay, I know how to do this.' But I don't know anything about babies. So this might be our thing, Ben's and mine."

Kathie was tongue-tied. Her sister with a houseful of teenagers?

"Hey, guys?" From across the room, Kim held up a pair of off-white sandals with a three-inch heel. "What about these?"

"I wouldn't make it down the aisle," Kate said.

Kim made a face. She loved high heels. "All right. I'll keep looking."

"You think I'm crazy, don't you?" Kate asked.

"It doesn't sound like anything I thought you'd ever do," Kathie said carefully.

"I know. I'm not saying we will. Ben just brought it up the other day, and…well, it just sounded right to me. You know how sometimes, you can be not even thinking of something, and then, someone mentions it, and it just feels right? It was like that. And there are so many kids Shannon's age who don't have a family, and have mostly given up on ever having one. It's just something we're going to think about. It's like, right now, everything is so good. Other than Jax going nuts and throwing Joe through the glass wall, I mean."

Miss Nancy gave a snort and told Kathie, "Pins going in. Don't move."

"Yes, ma'am."

Kate laughed. "I really am happy. I have a wonderful husband, and a new daughter and a job I love. Jax and Gwen are getting married. You're home. Kim's finally done with college, and she's home. It feels like…I can have anything now. Like anything is possible."

"That's great," Kathie said.

"Really, I mean it. And it's time for you to listen to me about this." Kate put a hand on her arm. "Don't run away—"

"She can't run away now. I'm not done," Miss Nancy said, and the look she gave Kathie had her wondering if Miss Nancy was in on a plan to keep Kathie cornered precisely for this reason.

"Listen and believe me," Kate said. "Ben is my guy. He's it. The one. I know it. I don't want anyone but him, and I never will. I can't even talk about him without blushing. It's like I get this silly little glow, just thinking about him. I am crazy in love with this man, and so happy, I can hardly believe it."

She stood there, truly glowing, in front of Kathie.

"But...what if you change your mind?" Kathie asked.

Kate laughed. "I'm not going to change my mind."

"You changed your mind about Joe," Kathie reminded her.

"No, I made a mistake with Joe."

"I'll say," Miss Nancy piped up. "Honey, if you can wait five years to marry a man, you might as well wait forever, because you obviously don't really want to marry him."

"She's right," Kate said.

Kathie stood there, trapped by her dress and a bossy woman with a ton of pins. She knew that her sister looked happy. It would have been impossible not to notice in the time Kathie had been home, that her sister seemed not only happy, but different. Softer. Kinder. At ease in every way. Oh, she could still get upset and still try to boss everyone around, when need be, like with Jax when he'd gone nuts.

But there was something fundamentally different about her.

Like everything was easier for her now. Like she'd been holding her breath for years, kind of holding the world as she knew it in place, and now she'd figured out how to exhale. That it was safe to let go of all that control she'd hung on to for so long and let things be. That she felt safe in doing so.

Because of the man she'd chosen so hastily six months ago?

"Just look at me," Kate said. "You know it's true. You know I'm happy."

"I want to believe that you are," Kathie said. "I want that so much, and I still feel awful about what happened—"

"Don't. Because I don't. Not at all. I wasn't supposed to marry Joe. I know that. And what happened between you and Joe just helped us realize we were making a mistake. If I hadn't done that, I wouldn't have found Ben. I wouldn't be married to him and ridiculously happy now. So I don't care what happened with you and Joe. I don't want you to feel bad about it for another second."

Kathie blinked back tears, ready to reach for her sister.

"Don't move," Miss Nancy barked.

"But—"

"Oh, it's perfect!" Gwen's gasp came from behind them. "Shannon, it's absolutely perfect!"

Miss Nancy finally released her, and Kathie turned to see Shannon in a shimmery ice-blue sheath, with a fitted bodice and a pencil-thin skirt that came all the way down to the floor. It made her look impossibly young and all grown up at the same time. She stood there awkwardly, frowning, uncomfortable, looking like she desperately wanted to hear they loved the dress as much as she did, but was afraid her own eyes were lying to her in the mirror.

It was hard to see the truth sometimes, even when it was right there in front of someone. Kathie turned and looked at her sister, who was beaming.

"Perfect," Kate said.

"Well, since they don't have any black leather in this place…" Shannon said, shrugging but not managing to infuse so much as an ounce of bravado in her voice. It was trembling with every word.

"Okay, you're right. The dress isn't perfect," Kate said. "But…it'll do."

"Nonsense, it's perfect," Gwen said.

Kate turned back to Kathie. "See. I have a perfect life. Just keep thinking about it. One day, it will all sink in."

"You think?"

Kate nodded. "Especially the fact that Joe is definitely available. He's perfectly free to do whatever he wants, and so are you. There's nothing standing in your way, if he's the person you really want."

"No. Joe will never be happy without you."

"Oh, honey," her sister said. "If he's ever going to be happy, it will have to be without me. And I think you should see what you can do about that. After all, I want you both to be happy."

Kathie gave up and let her tears fall. She'd worried they'd never truly get past this, and yet, she'd wanted so much to believe that they could. That things could go back to being the way they'd always been between her and her sister.

"I love you so much," Kathie said.

"Oh, honey." Kate grabbed her and hugged her.

"Hey, enough with the waterworks," Shannon yelled at them. "It's embarrassing!"

Kate shushed her, then looked back at Miss Nancy. "Do you think you could check Shannon's dress now? She won't stay in it for long, and it's the one we want."

"Just when things were getting good over here." Miss Nancy looked quite put out. But she gathered her things and headed for Shannon.

Kathie waited until the woman was gone, then whispered miserably to her sister, "Even if I did want him, he doesn't want me."

"You don't know that. You haven't given it any kind of real chance. And Joe's… well, it takes him a while to figure things out. He probably isn't done analyzing the whole mess from last year, and he'd want to analyze it half to death. The whole cycle of cause and effect is like a religion to him. His eyes and ears tell him one thing happened, but he'd predicted a completely different outcome, and he needs to understand why he was wrong."

"Okay, I know that about him."

"You'll have to be patient with him. Trust that what you're seeing right now isn't about you or any feelings he might have for you. It's just him still trying to make sense of things."

"So…you're like giving him to me?" Kathie couldn't believe it.

"If he was mine to give, I would."

Wow.

"I don't know what to say."

"You don't have to say anything," Kate said. "I just wanted you to know that I'm fine with anything that might develop between the two of you. You don't have to worry about Jax anymore. He's terrified you're going to leave town again. If it takes him butting out of your love life to make you stay, he'll do it. Kim just wants you here, no matter what, so she's not a problem, and as for the rest of the town…forget about them. Kathie, there's nothing left to stand in your way. If you want the man, it's time. Go get him."

Kathie gaped at her sister. "I…I can't do that!"

"Of course you can."

"He doesn't want me. Last year…you have to know, it was all me. Every bit of it."

Kate shook her head. "It couldn't possibly have been. This is Joe we're talking about. The most responsible, careful man in the world. If he hadn't felt a thing for you, he never would have kissed you."

"I kissed him. It was me."

"Kathie, if he hadn't had feelings for you, and you'd thrown yourself at him, he would have been surprised and embarrassed by it. He would have told you as kindly as possible that he was sorry if he'd ever given you reason to think there could be anything between the two of you, but that he was absolutely and completely in love with me, and nothing could ever change that. But he didn't do any of those things, did he?"

"No, but…he was just surprised, and he felt guilty."

"Guilty because he enjoyed it. Because he was kissing you back. When we finally broke up, and I finally asked him if there was someone else, do you know what he said to me?"

She shook her head, not wanting to know.

"He said he couldn't be engaged to me while he felt the way he did about another woman, and that woman was you. His big jumble of confusing feelings were all about you."

Kathie went quiet for a moment, thinking it through as best she could. "When I ran into him last week, he did say that he hasn't been thinking clearly lately."

"There you go. Poor guy. He's probably never

been confused about what he wants in his entire life. No wonder he's such a mess."

"And he seemed…really confused the day I met him at the bank before the fight he got into with Jax."

"Yes!"

"He kissed me, and…well, you know. You saw the pictures, didn't you?"

Kate nodded.

"I can't believe there are pictures!"

"Honey, forget about the pictures. He kissed you, and then what?"

"It was the way he did it," she said. "I gave him a peck on the cheek when I walked into the bank, because we were going to do our whole pretend-to-be-dating thing. But then he kissed me back, and it wasn't a peck on the cheek."

"Yes! What was it?"

"It was…slow. Like he moved in slow motion. Kind of like he was scared to get that close to me, but then when he did, he stayed there, like something reached out and grabbed him and held him there with his nose nuzzling my cheek, like he just couldn't pull away—"

"Yes!" Kate yelled, practically dancing in place. "I knew it!"

"What?" Kim called out from across the room, buried in shoes. "What's going on?"

"Nothing," they both claimed.

"I don't believe either one of you," she complained.

"Tell me everything, quick," Kate said, "Before her love of gossip outweighs her love of shoes." ·

"There's nothing to tell, really. Except it was... I didn't understand why he did it then or later, in the alley..."

"Yes, in the alley?"

"He kissed me again, when nobody was around, like he just had to do it."

"Ahhh!" Kate squealed and grabbed Kathie by the arms.

"What is it?" Kim said, arriving by their sides.

"Nothing," Kathie said. "Kate's just happy."

"I'm very happy!"

"Why?" Kim asked.

"Because we're all together, and our brother's getting married. Ben and I are about to officially have a daughter, and life is good. It's very, very good."

"What else?"

"That's not enough?" Kathie asked.

"No. There's something else going on." She turned to Kathie. "You must have done something again. You look guilty."

"Nothing happened," Kathie insisted.

"Wait! Are there pictures this time? Where's my cell phone. Maybe someone sent me the pictures, since no one else ever tells me anything about what's going on with my own family." She started digging in her purse.

"There are no more pictures," Kathie said.

Everyone had already seen them all.

Chapter Nine

Miss Punctuality was a dead bore.

She worked at the local high school, she said, as the senior records administrator, which Joe finally figured out meant she kept track of who was there and who wasn't every day.

She confessed to having never missed a day of school in her life, not when she was a student and certainly not as the senior records administrator.

Joe, having been taught it was polite to look for common ground with a woman on a date, had been forced to confess that he'd gone from kindergarten through twelfth grade with a perfect attendance record, as well.

That had her thinking they were soul mates already.

Joe frowned and took a bite of his steak. His mother had bugged him so much, he'd finally given in and gone out with Miss Punctuality. His face had healed. He wasn't walking with a limp anymore, and he hadn't seen Kathie or any member of the Cassidy clan in eight days.

He should be happy about that, but found it oddly unsettling instead.

And he wasn't happy to be out with Miss Punctuality.

She was...ordinary looking, with straight brown hair cut neatly just above her shoulders, a non-objectionable figure in brown slacks and a tan sweater. She had brown eyes and a nose that wasn't too big, not really, and she seemed to go through life with a very serious expression on her face.

She also seemed to think kids missing a day of school without a valid excuse should be horse-whipped.

"It's like students these days would have you believe the plague has hit," she told him, describing in grave detail the hordes of irresponsible school children she faced every day. "And you can't trust a word the brats say. I think they teach beginning forgery classes on the Internet these days. They can all do a reasonable facsimile of their parents' signatures. I've caught three this week alone who tried calling me on the phone, claiming to be their own parent, giving themselves an excused absence. Honestly, it's shocking the behaviors we have to deal with."

Joe nodded, hoping for an expression that seemed sympathetic. "What is it, a week from the end of school here?"

She nodded. "The worst time of the year. The absolute worst!"

And it had been eighty degrees and sunny all week.

It had given him odd thoughts of skipping out of work early himself.

Come to think of it, he didn't believe he'd ever missed a day of work at the bank, either. Sick days were for wimps, right? Vacations? He thought he'd taken a few of those, but he'd earned them. Sick days were for the sick, and Joe was never sick.

He wondered if Marta would be able to tell if he was lying if he tried calling in sick tomorrow, if the weather was nice? She'd probably faint first, he decided, because he never took a sick day. Or with her imagination run amok, as it tended to do lately, she'd have him being either suicidal or homicidal over the scandal of the recent bank brawl. She was still worried he was going to get fired.

Miss Punctuality was checking her watch, informing him that it had been a full five and a half minutes since they'd last seen their waiter, which was simply unacceptable.

"What do you need?" he asked. "I'll find someone to take care of it."

"I don't need anything. It's just the principle of the thing. I might have needed something, and then, where would our waiter have been? Not here? He probably skipped school regularly. That's what happens to these kids. They never learn responsibility."

Joe nodded, smiled faintly and listened as she told him about the computer program she'd adapted specifically for keeping track of individual students and the excuses they'd used in claiming officially excused absences from school.

"Before I put this program in place, a full fifteen percent of the school's population had already claimed to have attended the funerals of more than four grandmothers or grandfathers in the time they've been in high school" she said, obviously pleased with herself.

"Well, there are a lot of children of blended families these days," Joe said.

"Yes, but the odds of any student having and losing four grandparents within a four-year span are astronomical. I assure you, I calculated the whole thing out."

"Oh." Surely she could have a lot more fun in Vegas, calculating odds on the roulette wheel or at blackjack. Not that he could imagine her in Vegas.

"Numbers are a wonderful thing," she said, beaming. "Don't you agree?"

"Well…" He always had taken a certain pleasure

in all the rules of mathematics. The patterns, the equations, probabilities and statistics.

It just all struck him as so dull right now.

Maybe it was her glee in trying to tamp down on the senior's upcoming skip day, an unauthorized but traditional time for them to break free from classes one last day before graduation. It was set for the following day, expected to be an absolutely perfect one weather-wise.

His class had celebrated Senior Skip Day, too. Naturally, he'd gone to school. No blowing a perfect attendance record at the last minute.

He wished now that he'd taken the day off.

Nobody cared that he'd never missed a day of school or work.

Except Miss Punctuality.

"I'm so glad we did this," she said. "Your mother has been bragging about you to my mother for months."

Joe smiled. He was never listening to his mother again.

Maybe this was why Kate fell out of love with him. Because he was boring, spouted off statistics at the drop of a hat and his work was boring. Not that Kate didn't love numbers, herself, but still…

Was Joe this boring?

He hoped not.

"Would you excuse me for just a moment?" he asked, getting to his feet, because he felt like if he sat here and listened to her for one more minute, he was going to choke or something. "I'll be right back."

He headed in the direction of the bathroom, but ended up in the bar instead finally able to breathe easier, but still uneasy, unsettled, unhappy if he were being completely truthful with himself.

On sheer impulse alone, he ordered a shot of whiskey, straight up, because when he got to the bar that's what the man next to him had just ordered, and he looked like a guy who'd never spout statistics to a date or anyone else.

Joe picked up the tiny shot glass and drained it, wincing as it hit the back of his throat.

He was losing it.

Nothing in his life made sense anymore.

Nothing worked.

Old patterns, old habits, old things that normally brought him comfort… it was like the world had changed around him, and he'd missed it completely. Like someone had taken his old life away in the blink of an eye. He kept trying to find it, to get it back, but he just couldn't.

And he didn't understand anything about this strange, new world in which he found himself.

"Want another one, bud?" the bartender asked, looking down at the empty glass in Joe's hand.

He frowned, thought about it, then…dammit, he could swear he heard *that* voice.

Her voice.

"Joe? Are you all right?"

He turned around, and there she was, staring at him.

And he felt a surge of emotions at the sight of her, a horrible, overwhelming mishmash of things. Dread, because things so often went bad when she was close. Happiness, because he'd felt like he was suffocating back there with Miss Punctuality. Utter confusion, because he had no idea what to do with Kathie, but he feared he'd missed her terribly.

God, help him.

"What's the matter?" she said.

"I'm on the first date from hell," he whispered, then wanted to kick himself for the kick of hurt that flashed through her eyes.

Dammit.

He really didn't want to hurt her. Not ever.

And so often, that's exactly what he found himself doing.

"I thought some of the gossip about you and me might die down a little if I gave in and took out my mother's friend's daughter," he said, trying to explain.

"Oh," Kathie said, chin back up, expression carefully guarded once again.

Joe decided brutal honesty about the date was the only way to go.

"Miss Punctuality, I call her. She's probably got

a stop watch on me right now, because she'd have an idea of how long one could possibly be away from the dinner table without being rude, and she'd want to keep track of how I did on the first-date-rudeness scale. She keeps track of everything."

"Really?" Kathie didn't look quite so sad.

Joe nodded. "She's the attendance clerk at the high school. I swear, if she could convince someone to buy her a polygraph machine, she'd strap the students in and start questioning every one of them who claimed they needed to go to the dentist for the afternoon."

Kathie's mouth started to twitch, and there was a twinkle of amusement in her eyes. "Well…hers is not a fun job."

"Mine isn't, either, but I hope I'm not so fanatical about it."

"I thought you loved your job."

"I do," he said, then had to reconsider. He thought he had. He'd been proud to be promoted to bank president at such a young age, and he'd worked hard. But loved it?

It was a challenge. It was hard. It was something he could do well.

Surely he had loved it. He'd spent eight years there, after all.

"I think I still do. I'm not exactly sure," he admitted. "Maybe I'm still in that weird place."

"Oh."

"I don't like it here," he said.

"This restaurant? I always thought it was very good."

"No, this weird place in my head. I don't like it."

Kathie blinked up at him like she had absolutely no idea what to say to him, or maybe it was that look that said she wasn't quite sure she even knew him anymore.

He barely recognized himself these days.

He had the oddest urge at times to go stand in front of a mirror and stare at himself, to see if he still looked like him, if there was anything on the outside that looked different. It seemed he should look different on the outside, because he felt so different on the inside. He simply wasn't the same anymore.

And he was having trouble breathing again. That awful choking feeling was back. Thoughts were running through his head at breakneck speed, and the next thing he knew, one of the most unsettling ones just popped out.

"Do you ever look at yourself in the mirror and wonder who you are?" he asked.

"Joe, how many of these have you had?" Kathie asked, gently taking the empty shot glass from him and putting it on the bar behind him.

The man sitting on the barstool to the right laughed out loud at that.

Joe glared at him. If Kathie hadn't walked in

when she did, Joe would probably be having this conversation with that guy.

"Just one," he said.

"Okay," Kathie said, taking Joe by the arm and turning him around. "I think we've spent enough time in the bar."

"No. Really. I only had one. I don't get drunk. You know that. It's just that nothing I do or say makes sense to me anymore, so I'm not surprised that it wouldn't make sense to you or anyone else. No wonder people keep looking at me funny. I don't make any sense. I can't seem to hide it anymore. My own mother thinks I'm nuts."

He finally stopped talking, way too late.

"She does?" Kathie asked with a gentle smile, like she was indulging a three-year-old who was about to have a fit.

"Yes. And she thinks it's all your fault."

"Oh. Great."

"She thinks you're dangerous."

Kathie laughed.

"To me," he said. "That I do crazy things when you're around."

She stopped in midstride, turned to face him and put her palms flat against his chest to stop him in his tracks, way too close to her.

"What do you think, Joe? Am I bad for you? Am I dangerous?"

"I don't know how you could be," he said.

"You're Kathie Cassidy. You're Kate's little sister. I still think of you as a teenager. It's like a part of you never grew up, where I was concerned. But then, there's this other part that's...well, that's not Kate's little sister. The part that's a woman I don't even know."

The one who'd kissed him with so much longing and sadness, with so much aching need the day her mother had died, and had just blown him away with everything she made him feel, everything she made him want. Things that he knew were completely wrong, because of who he was and who she was, but things he'd felt nonetheless.

Things he still felt whenever he got too close to her.

Like right now.

"I can't put the two of you together in my head, the girl I've always known and the other one...the woman," he said. "I can't begin to make sense of you. I keep hoping I can just stop trying, but it all keeps coming back, and I never know what to do about it."

He had his hands on her arms by then, stroking lightly from her shoulders to her elbows, trying not to grab her and pull her even closer. Not here in the bar when he was on a date with Miss I-Need-A-Polygraph-Machine.

But Kathie...it was like she'd slipped inside his head, filled his thoughts, his senses and left him in a fog of nothing but wanting and needing her. And he'd fought it for so long. It just never went away.

"Make it stop," he all but begged Kathie.

"I would if I could, Joe. I did for the longest time, and then I just couldn't anymore. I'm sorry. I don't know how," she said, then pressed her mouth to his.

He was glad she didn't know how, glad she didn't stop.

She sank into him, and he anchored her there with hands that caught her and held her against him while he was absolutely dizzy from the sweet, now familiar taste of her.

His downfall.

His utter ruin.

His way to madness.

He feared he was devouring her, right there in the bar. There would probably be pictures, but what was a man to do? The whole town was armed and dangerous where they were concerned.

Let them take all the pictures they wanted to.

He just kept kissing her, a bizarre sense of rightness coursing through him with every quickening beat of his heat.

He wasn't confused at the moment. His head wasn't spinning.

He was just happy.

Joyous, even.

There was nothing to think about but her, and how

much he'd wanted this, despite how hard he'd resisted.

The image of the girl he'd known was falling away, replaced by all the things she made him feel and the fact that he wasn't engaged anymore. Everyone already knew everything they'd done, so there was simply nothing left to lose.

Only things to gain.

This feeling, mainly.

This joy.

Kathie and her mouth and her soft, sweet scent, her arms around his neck, her hands in his hair, the warm weight of her body against his.

He didn't care if he was crazy.

This was what he wanted, what he—

"Ahhhhh!"

A loud sputtering sound of outrage managed to cut through his passion-fogged brain, and he broke off the kiss, lifted his head and there, standing in the bar in front of him and Kathie was…

Miss Punctuality glaring at them both.

This was bad on so many levels, Joe realized.

It was terribly rude and disrespectful, both to his date and to Kathie, which he tried to never be. It was something Kathie's brother was more likely to do, before he met his fiancé, than anything anyone would ever believe of Joe.

And yet, here he was, caught kissing one woman

while out with another, yet another first for him to add to his life experiences.

"I was going to see if you'd gotten lost," Miss Punctuality said. "But I see that you didn't. You were simply…distracted for seven minutes and thirty-four seconds. So distracted that you forgot about the fact that you were having dinner with me."

"I am so sorry," Joe said.

She held up a hand to stop him right there, not wanting to hear it.

"Hi, Winnie," Kathie said, looking chagrined.

"Kathie," Miss Punctuality growled.

"You two know each other?" Joe asked.

Kathie nodded. "I had a couple of long-term substitute teaching positions at the high school before I got my job at the middle school two years ago."

"And was shockingly lax about submitting her class attendance rolls while she was at my school," Winnie complained.

"Yeah," Kathie said. "Sorry about that, too."

"So," the woman turned back to Joe. "Everything I've heard about you and put down as ridiculous gossip is true? You two can't keep your hands off each other?"

"I'm trying. Really. I'm trying so hard," Joe said, then looked at Kathie, afraid she'd be hurt by that or insulted, justifiably so, and instead, saw that she was holding her sides and had clamped her mouth shut, trying not to bust out laughing.

"You think this is funny?" Winnie asked.

"No. I mean…I shouldn't," Kathie admitted, her shoulders shaking. "Really. I know I shouldn't—"

"Well, I guess you would. I mean, if you'd steal him from your own sister, I can see where you wouldn't hesitate to steal him from anyone else."

"Winnie, it's your first date with him. It's not like you own him. I mean, I am sorry. It was rude of us, but don't make it out to be a tragedy."

Winnie glared at Kathie some more, then turned to Joe. "Your mother will hear all about this from my mother."

Joe just stood there. He'd never imagined having two women fight over him. It seemed to be a common male fantasy, but it had never been his. More Kathie's brother's style, once again. Although Jax seemed to come out of situations like this where the women still liked him somehow. That part baffled Joe completely.

Winnie looked like she hated him, this after one date. Granted, it was ending badly, but still, as Kathie had pointed out, it was one date.

"I am really sorry," he began again.

"Oh, shut up, Joe."

She grabbed a drink off a table next to her and threw it in his face.

Kathie tried to be pragmatic about the whole thing.

It was just one more little public scene that would be gossiped about all over town.

What was one more?

Her brother had been sworn to silence on all things related to her love life, so they didn't have to worry about him flipping out and making a scene or throwing Joe through any more walls.

Plus, Winnie was gone. She'd stalked out after tossing the drink on Joe.

Okay.

Kathie took a fortifying breath, trying to steady herself.

Nothing to do but move on with her plan.

The go-after-Joe plan, one which she felt completely inadequate to carry out.

Now or never, she told herself.

She certainly wasn't going to spend another five years of her life in guilt-inducing longing for him, but never acting on it.

She grabbed a rolled up cloth napkin from an empty table at her side and started dabbing at the wine that was dripping off Joe's chin and his nose, even his earlobe, and tried not to laugh.

"It's red, isn't it?" he asked.

She nodded.

"I hate red wine."

"And this is one of your favorite shirts. I've seen you in it a dozen times."

"I don't have favorites," he claimed. "I have a rotation. A regular rotation of shirts, so that they wear evenly. It sounds completely ridiculous when I say it now, but that's what I do with my shirts."

"Okay," Kathie said, pressing the cloth to the worst of the stains on his shirt. "You have a shirt plan."

"I have a plan for everything. Or…I used to. I don't anymore."

"Well, sometimes you have to make new plans," Kathie tried to tell him.

He looked like the idea frightened him.

"Come on, Joe. What would you do if you had to make a new plan?"

"I have no idea. Except that it's not good to make plans when you can't think straight, which I can't seem to manage to do these days. So I'm sure this is not the time for a new plan."

"How about starting with something small, like a one-day plan, and then you could move on to more long-term stuff. If you were going to do nothing but plan your day tomorrow, what would you want to do?"

"I was thinking of taking the day off. Claiming a sick day and playing hooky instead. She made me want to do that. Your friend Winnie."

Kathie frowned. "She would never play hooky with anybody."

"I know. I wasn't going with her. She just made me want to get away. It's supposed to be really nice. The weather lately has been perfect. I was thinking of spending part of the day at the falls."

"It's awfully close to the bank, Joe. I don't know

if that's a good idea. Someone would e-mail Marta a dozen photos of you out enjoying yourself when you were supposed to be home sick."

"I don't care," he said. "I like the falls. Do you like the falls?"

"Yes." Was he asking her on a date? To the best known, most public place in town, other than the bank or the diner at noon?

"How do you feel about red wine?" he asked.

"I like it."

She barely got the words out, and then he was kissing her again, his lips tasting of the wine, his shirt beneath her hands wet with the wine, the stains no doubt soaking into her own blouse. Not that she cared.

She kissed him and tasted the sweet tartness of the wine, kissed him with complete abandon and need.

It didn't seem like he cared anymore, either, that he was supposed to stay away from her or that he wanted to stay away from her. Just that he was here with her and wanted to stay.

Chapter Ten

Kathie came home an hour and fifteen minutes later, wine-soaked and humming, to find her sisters and Gwen in the living room, huddled around the coffee table addressing wedding invitations, which she was supposed to be helping with.

"Have a little wine with your dinner?" Gwen asked.

She looked down at her once-white blouse, stained a reddish pink from the wine. "Just a bit." She held up a bag of takeout. "I brought food. Sorry it took so long. They were...slow tonight."

"That's fine," Kate said. "See anyone we know at the restaurant?"

"A few people," she admitted, setting the bag

down on the little table in the corner and pulling out Styrofoam containers of food.

"You know, I heard the oddest thing at school the other day. I heard that Joe was taking Winnie Fitzgerald to dinner tonight," Kim said, making her way to the table to find her chicken salad.

"Winnie Fitzgerald?" Kate said.

Kim nodded. "She was at the high school when I was a student there. She always frightened me when I had to miss school."

"She scares me, too," Gwen said, finding her own salad. "She comes in the flower shop all the time. She takes care of the flower fund for the teachers and everyone who works at the high school, and she always acts like she's afraid we're going to cheat her out of a dime or a nickel or something when she buys flowers. This after she complains about the price of everything."

"Poor Joe," Kate said, serious as could be. "Someone should save him from Winnie."

Kathie looked from one seemingly innocent face to another, not buying their act at all. "Let me guess. There are pictures, and you guys already saw them?"

All three of them burst out laughing.

Kathie knew she'd made a spectacle of herself. And it was a terrible thing to do—grab another woman's date and kiss him like that. She still couldn't believe she'd done it.

Her mother would have been appalled.

She'd just gotten a little crazy, thinking after all these years of wanting Joe that someone else would swoop in like that and steal him from her.

Not that he belonged to Kathie in any way.

"So, we heard that Winnie just threw a glass of wine in Joe's face," Gwen said, still laughing. "Did she throw another one at you?"

"No," Kathie said.

"You spilled wine on yourself?" Kim tried.

"No."

"Then how did it get all over you?"

"It's the same one Winnie threw at Joe," Kathie admitted.

"So, you were standing pretty close together at the time?"

"No," Kathie said.

They looked puzzled for a moment, then Kate started to get it, then Gwen, nodding knowingly.

"Wait a minute," Kim said, still confused.

"Think about it," Gwen said, turning to Kim. "The kiss came after Winnie dumped the wine on him?"

"No. I mean…yes. I mean…there was one before, and one after. Maybe more than one after. Kisses, I mean."

Kim shook her head. "Joe would not be hiding out in the bar kissing one woman while he was on a date with another one."

"It wasn't his fault," Kathie said. "It was me. I

grabbed him and kissed him before he could even stop me. Plus, he's confused."

"Oh, good," Kate said, and the other two looked at her like she must be as nutty as Joe at the moment.

Kim was watching the three of them like she wasn't sure she was really okay with this, but might take her cue from Kate, who did seem unconcerned.

"You guys sent me there for takeout knowing Joe was going to be there with Winnie?" Kathie asked.

"No," Kim said.

"You might not have," Gwen admitted. "But Kate and I did."

"Ahhh!" Kathie groaned. "You two!"

"We're not going to let Winnie Fitzgerald get her hands on him. I like Joe too much to ever let something like that happen to him," Kate said. "Besides, I thought it might…inspire you to do something, which it obviously did, which is good. It was good, wasn't it? I mean, you don't get that much wine on yourself if it wasn't good."

"Well…I guess…" Kathie blushed. "Yes."

The three of them giggled once more.

"So, what's next? You need a plan," Kate said.

"I don't have a plan. I just have…I guess you could call it a date."

She was terrified, actually.

She and Joe were going on a date.

A real one.

Then she thought of something.

"You guys have to keep Jax away from the falls tomorrow at noon, just in case the truce doesn't hold. Joe's taking me on a picnic."

Joe was bare-chested, standing in his kitchen soaking his shirt in a lame attempt to get the wine out of it, when his doorbell rang that evening.

He had a terrible fear that it would be his mother.

He'd thought of pulling his car around to the back of his house when he came home from the restaurant, just so that if she came by, he might get away with pretending not to be there. But that was cowardly, and he was thirty-one years old. It was unseemly to be so worried about hearing what his mother thought of him.

Leaving the shirt in the sink, he went to answer the door, and sure enough, there she was. *Mom.*

Her eyes got big and round as she stared at his bare chest, and then she whispered, "Is that girl here?"

"No, Mother."

"Well!" She took a breath and said, "I cannot believe you would shame me this way. And with that nice girl, Winnie."

Joe turned around and headed back to the kitchen and his ruined shirt, knowing she'd follow. "Winnie is not a nice girl. She's a very unhappy woman."

"Which is no excuse for your behavior," his

mother called after him. "That awful girl practically attacks you in the restaurant—"

"Kathie didn't attack me. She kissed me. I kissed her back. Quite happily."

"And you take her side against poor Winnie's?"

"Poor Winnie doused me with wine before I had a chance to do much of anything."

"Except kiss that troublesome girl, right there in the same restaurant where you'd taken poor Winnie to dinner!"

"Yeah," Joe said, picking up his sopping wet shirt and wringing the water out of it. "That's what I did. Sorry. I shouldn't have let you talk me into going out with Winnie Fitzgerald—"

"She is exactly the sort of girl you should be seeing. A nice girl—"

"No, Mother. Listen. I'm not saying it again. She's a miserable, unhappy, petty, judgmental woman, and I don't want to have anything to do with her."

His mother gasped, then looked appalled, then simply defeated. "What am I going to do with you? All these years, you've been no trouble at all. The perfect son. The most wonderful one any mother could want, and now…Joe! You know how things were after your father ran off with that awful woman."

"I do," Joe said. "And I'm sorry. But I'm not my father."

"People are talking about you and that awful girl the same way they did about your father and that woman he ran off with."

"I know it may feel like that to you, but it's just not true. I'm not married to anyone. I don't have children. And I'm not running off with someone else's wife. There's no comparison. Now, if you're saying I have to live my life always conscious of what people in this town think and trying to win their approval, to make life more pleasant for you, well…I'm sorry, Mom. I can't do that anymore. I'm done."

"Done with what? Being respectable?"

"Being unhappy. Being bored. Being too worried about doing the absolute right thing all the time to ever let myself simply do something for fun."

His mother looked horrified. "This girl is going to ruin you," she claimed.

"You think so? I'm starting to think she's going to save me."

Kathie felt almost like a criminal, sneaking into the park to meet Joe the next day. She was so nervous she was shaking and felt like everyone who saw her knew she must be up to something illicit.

Much as she wanted a chance with Joe, she still felt guilty about being with him and wondered if the feeling would ever go away, sisterly approval or no sisterly approval. Kim was even coming around.

"I do think Kate's happy," she'd conceded, right before she'd left that morning. "I never thought she could be without Joe, but now…"

That was huge, as far as Kathie was concerned.

"So…you're not mad at me anymore?" she'd asked.

"Well…it's still a little weird…the idea of you and Joe. But…I guess if Kate's okay with it, who am I to be mad about it?"

Kathie had grabbed her and hugged her so hard, Kim had protested that she was having trouble breathing. She'd never thought to win both her sisters' approval. Now, if only they could get Jax to not just be silent about the whole thing, but be…what was the best they could hope for between him and Joe? Cordial? Was that too much?

Kathie didn't know.

She just hoped Gwen did her part and kept Jax away.

It was indeed a beautiful spring day. The sun was out. There wasn't a cloud in the sky. Flowers were blooming. The grass was lush and green. Birds were singing, literally.

Kathie was nervous, but feeling something very close to happy.

Better than happy, actually.

Giddy.

She was practically giddy.

She spotted Joe sitting on a bench near the river, overlooking the falls. He was wearing a pair of jeans and a polo shirt, looking oddly unfamiliar without his trademark suit and tie.

He saw her, stood up and smiled, holding up a picnic basket.

Butterflies started rioting in Kathie's stomach.

Her fantasies of a romance between her and Joe had never gotten this specific, down to them having an actual date. To what he'd say to her, and what she'd say to him, and how she'd act. She was so nervous, she had to fight the ridiculous urge to turn and run in the other direction.

Her and Joe? The reality of where they stood at this moment—on the brink of having a real relationship—was almost too much for her to handle.

She stumbled a bit as she walked toward him, and he rushed forward to catch her and keep her from falling. Which meant, she ended up much closer to him, right from the start, than she expected.

"Hi," she whispered, caught there and unable to do anything else.

"Hi," he said, looking a bit uneasy himself.

Were they going to be terrified of each other for life?

"You look…different," he said.

"Different, good? Or different, bad?"

"Good. Definitely good. Just…oh, hell, I don't know." He frowned. "I haven't been on a date with anyone but your sister or Winnie in years."

He looked so pained upon saying it that Kathie started to laugh, and then he did, too. Things were going to be awkward, but they could work around that.

Kathie stretched up on her toes and kissed him on the cheek, smiling as she drew back, a little surprised at how forward she'd managed to become but not at all sorry about getting to kiss him.

"I think I should warn you—if someone spots us and calls my mother, and she gets here in time to make a fuss, just get behind me and let me fight her off, okay? She's my problem, not yours."

"You're worried that she'd hurt me?" Kathie asked.

"No, worried about what she might say. I should have brought tape for her mouth. I'll pick her up and haul her to her car, if I have to. If she ever starts working together with your brother, we're in real trouble."

"Surely if I can handle Winnie, I can handle your mother," Kathie reasoned.

"I just don't want her to upset you," he said.

Which was sweet, Kathie decided.

She liked the idea of him wanting to take care of her, even if it meant duct taping his mother's mouth shut, throwing her over his shoulder and hauling her away.

"I suppose the idea of us having anything resembling a normal date is too much to ask, at least anywhere in this town," she said.

They picked a spot for their picnic, a bluff overlooking the waterfall. Joe spread the blanket he'd brought, and they sat down. He started unpacking the food, and Kathie helped.

"So, how do you like playing hooky?"

"I think it's a shame I waited until I was thirty-one to try it for the first time," he said. "You should have heard Marta when I called in sick. She wanted to call an ambulance to come take me to the hospital. She was sure I must be deathly ill, and when I tried to assure her that I wasn't, she decided the scene at the restaurant with Winnie must have been much worse than she'd heard. That I must have a concussion or some other dire injury from the altercation in the bar."

Kathie grinned.

She could grin about altercations in bars, couldn't she? Because she really didn't care, except to feel a little guilty about hurting Winnie's feelings.

Joe pulled a tiny bottle of red wine, one that couldn't have more than two glasses of wine in it, out of the picnic basket and put it on the blanket between them.

"I thought you didn't like red?"

"Changed my mind," he claimed.

Which had her thinking of it being all over him, even on his lips, when she'd kissed him in the restaurant the night before.

Would he be kissing her here in the park on their picnic, too?

She felt a wave of heat all over just thinking about it.

When other girls had been in the full throes of first loves, first serious relationships, first sexual relationships, she'd been caught up in nothing but guilt-invoking dreams of him. Impossible dreams of him. Paralyzing dreams of him.

There'd simply never been anyone else.

Not that she hadn't tried to make herself forget him or even at times, make do with someone who wasn't him. But it had simply never worked.

He'd been the only one she'd ever wanted, and it was still nearly impossible for her to believe he was done with Kate, that Kate was done with him, and had all but handed him to Kathie on a silver platter.

The possibilities made her head spin.

Joe opened the wine, poured her a glass and one for himself, then took a sip and frowned.

"What's wrong?" Kathie asked.

"It's not quite the same way I remember it," he said, a slight smile on his face and an intent look in his eyes, one that sent another flash of heat through her whole body.

He was flirting with her.

Kathie gaped at him.

He'd never flirted with her! Never, ever, ever.

She didn't think she'd ever seen him flirt with Kate. It just wasn't something Joe Reed did.

When she continued to gape at him, he started looking unsure of himself and then worried and then…

"No. Wait," she said. She wanted him to flirt with her, even if it had thrown her for a moment. She wanted him happy and with wine on his lips and wine on her, and their mouths pressed together. She wanted all of these things, and she wasn't letting them slip away, not one moment of this wonderful, unbelievable chance they'd been given.

Kathie threw back a gulp of her wine, put her glass down and reached for him, all but launching herself into his arms.

He grinned and caught her close. "I have no idea what I'm doing here," he confessed.

"Me, either," she said. "But you could kiss me, and we could see how that works for us. I mean… that's worked before. I'm thinking it will work again and be fine. Just fine."

"Let's shoot for better than fine," he said, easing back onto the blanket and taking her with him, until they were lying on their sides, arm in arm.

He finally touched his lips to hers, and she could taste the wine between them. She'd never drink a drop of wine without thinking of this day with him.

His mouth moved over hers. Hers opened to his, and then it was like her whole body was humming with something that seemed to sparkle like glitter. She felt sparkly and floaty and ravenous, all at the same time.

The sun was warm on her back, and he was warm beside her and beneath. She thought there were birds singing somewhere, and could hear the sound of water rushing over the falls and far-off laughter from other people somewhere in the park.

They were, no doubt, making a spectacle of themselves, but she didn't care.

There was nothing to stand in their way anymore. She'd hidden her feelings and denied them for too long where he was concerned.

Just love me a little bit, she thought. Just a little bit. That would be enough. What she felt would more than balance things out.

He was lying half on his side, half on his back, and she was lying beside him and kind of on top of him, her hair loose and falling onto his face. He took both of his hands and pushed it away so he could kiss her again, then held the sides of her face in his hands.

"I'm afraid we spilled the wine," he said, grinning.

Kathie looked at his right shoulder and laughed. It was stained a reddish pink, just as his shirt and her blouse had been the night before.

"So, this is going to be one of those messy relationships," she said.

Feeling particularly daring, she reached for the little dessert container, opened it and found some kind of pie with a bit of whipped cream on top.

Joe lay stretched out on his back, waiting and watching to see what she was going to do.

"How do you feel about whipped cream?" she asked.

"I like it. You?"

She nodded, stuck her index finger into the whipped cream, touched it to his mouth, then smeared it across his lips, thinking she'd kiss it off of him. But he surprised her when his tongue touched the side of her finger, as gentle as a whisper, and lapped at the whipped cream there.

She couldn't move.

Hers was the body of a twenty-four-year-old woman that had done nothing but fantasize about him for years, and nothing in her imagination had come close to the reality of this day with him.

She started trembling all over, sensations rioting within her.

He pulled her face back down to his, and then he was kissing her once again.

She was starting to get scared.

Much as she wanted him, she could tell that if he wanted to strip her naked and have her—right there on the river banks in the park—she didn't think she'd try to stop him.

Not that Joe Reed would ever do anything like that.

But still…she had no defenses here.

Not against him.

So there was joy and longing and a new, terrible kind of fear.

Everyone had life-changing moments, and it seemed she was facing one with Joe.

It would work out, or it wouldn't.

The next few weeks, the next few months, and she would know.

She'd have everything she ever wanted, or she wouldn't.

It was almost too much to bear.

Chapter Eleven

They kissed until they scared each other half to death—it felt so good. Ate, then kissed some more. In truth, it was more like they were necking in the park in the middle of town in the middle of the day.

Not the kind of behavior anyone would ever expect from Kathie and certainly not from Joe. She had no idea who might have seen them. She'd been too caught up in how it had felt to care.

When it was over, her once-white shirt had grass stains on the back, where they'd rolled onto the grass at one point, and wine on the front, where she'd gotten too close to Joe and the wine that had soaked into his shirt then soaked into hers.

Her hair was mussed. She had no lip gloss left

and just hoped she could get home and changed before anyone else who knew her saw her in this state.

The landlady, who was eighty if she was a day, just happened to be watering the flowers in the planters on the front porch when Kathie walked in.

"Hello, Mrs. O'Connor," Kathie said, pasting on a smile.

"Oh, dear. Were you in an accident of some sort?"

"No." All flustered, Kathie couldn't think of anything else to say, so she just smiled and tried to play it off. "Just a lunch date. Bye."

The puzzled look on the woman's face said it all.

Kathie did not look like someone who'd been on a lunch date.

Oh, well.

She hurried down the hall and upstairs, passing her next-door neighbor, Lizzie Watson, on the way. Lizzie was in the high school chorus for four years with Kathie, and she was now teaching music at one of the local elementary schools.

She gave Kathie an odd look, then said, "What does the other guy look like?"

"Happy," Kathie said.

Because it was true. Kind of. Joe had looked happy a good bit of the time. And then he'd looked confused, and then maybe as worried as Kathie felt, for reasons she couldn't begin to know. She could guess they might be the same as hers, that the things she felt might be happening between them with lightning speed had the power to terrify her. But she couldn't be sure.

Joe had never been an easy guy to read.

Kathie got to her door, went to put her key in the lock, but found she didn't need to. The knob turned on its own, and then there she was, inside her apartment, which happened to be filled with her entire family.

Both sisters, Ben, Jax and his fiancée, all piled into their tiny living room in what looked like a family meeting. Gwen in the nearest chair, Jax by her side. Kate and Ben on the couch, along with Kim.

Kathie wanted to run in the other direction, but it wouldn't do any good. They were here, and they'd already seen her, no doubt already come up with all sorts of explanations for why she looked the way she did.

She wondered if they'd seen pictures yet.

"Hi," she said, walking slowly into the living room.

They all just stared at first.

She fought and lost the urge to smooth down her hair, which suddenly felt like it was going every which way, and then when she did, her hand caught on something. She tugged, and it came loose.

A little twig or something.

She frowned at it, then dropped it on the hallway table beside her.

Kate reached over and pulled out another. "You missed one," she said helpfully.

Kathie took that one, too, and put it aside, her cheeks burning.

Jax, to her left, sitting on the arm of Gwen's chair, sniffed and asked, "Wine again?"

Kathie nodded.

"Joe on another date with Winnie?" he asked.

"No. With me." She kept her head high. "And you promised not to say anything about anything, remember?"

"Just trying to be clear that it was a date, not a mugging, because I'd be entitled to say something about a mugging."

"I was not mugged," Kathie clarified.

"Ooooo-kay," he said, drawling out the word.

"Jax!" Kate and Gwen said together.

"Okay. All done. Nothing more from me. Of course, if either one of you have anything to say…"

"I've never known Joe to be clumsy. Or messy," Kate said, grinning. "But Kathie doesn't have to tell us anything she doesn't want to."

"Thank you. I have nothing to say," she claimed, then looking around the room, changed her mind. "Well, actually…please tell me this family meeting isn't about me and Joe."

"Could we do that?" Jax asked. "Have a family meeting about her and him? I'll be quiet. The rest of you can talk."

"No," Kate and Gwen said again.

"You don't have anything to say, Ben?" Jax tried. "I mean, you can't want the guy around? Not after what he did to Kate last year—"

"He didn't do anything to me," Kate insisted. "I was the one who broke up with him."

"You did not!" Kim said.

"I was there," Kate said. "I think I know what happened. I'm the one who broke up with him."

"She took one look at me, and that was it," Ben claimed, grinning as he came to stand beside her, his arm around her, tucking her against his side.

Kate rolled her eyes dramatically, but then she went and ruined the whole effect by kissing him and grinning right back at him.

"Okay, that's pretty much how it happened," Kate admitted, then turned to their brother. "And you? You weren't even surprised when I told you Joe and I had broken up. You acted like you knew all along it was coming, so for you to be outraged about it now—"

"Wait," Kathie said, turning to her brother. "What does she mean, you knew it was coming?"

"I suspected," he admitted.

"You did?" Kim said, obviously puzzled.

"Yeah, I did. So what?"

"Because you knew?" Kathie could hardly get the words out. "You already knew about Joe and me?"

"No," her brother said. "I would have kicked his butt if I'd known about you and him."

"Or thrown him through a glass wall?" Gwen asked, then started laughing.

Kate joined her, then Kim. Kathie smiled, as did Ben.

"Okay, okay. It wasn't one of my finer moments. Nobody messes with my little sisters," Jax said. "Or my wife-to-be."

"You promised you'd leave Joe alone," Kathie said.

"He will. And just to show there are no hard feelings, and that we can all get along with each other, I invited him to the wedding," Gwen said.

Jax's head whipped around. "You did what?"

"I invited him to my wedding," she repeated. "If you want to be there and marry me, you can come, too. If not—"

"Our wedding?" Jax complained.

"Don't worry," Ben said. "You'll be too nervous to notice who's there."

"I am not nervous."

"You will be," Ben claimed. "But we'll get you through it."

"Were you nervous?" Gwen asked Ben.

"Not about whether Kate and I were doing the right thing." He kissed her softly, sweetly. "I was nervous that she might decide it was crazy to be marrying me after only knowing me for three months."

"Me, too," Kim said.

"Me, three," Jax agreed.

"But mostly that day, I just wanted it done," Ben said, grinning down at Kate. "It's like you can see everything you want for your life, and it's right there in front of you, and you just want all the things that make it real, make it forever—you want those done. It's like it can't happen fast enough."

Kate wrapped her arms around him and kissed him soundly, right there in the living room in front of them all. When she pulled away, she was absolutely beaming.

"Speaking of which, it's been six whole months today," Ben said.

"And people said it wouldn't last." Kate laughed.

"Wait a minute," Kathie said, sensing something else that might be going on between them. "You're not…I mean, this meeting, it's not about…you said at the dress shop that you weren't pregnant."

Ben looked scared for a moment.

Kate laughed. "I'm not."

"Phew," Ben said, taking a breath. "I mean… we're still too freaked out being there when Shannon had her baby last fall. We may have been scarred for life by the experience. Although we are adding onto our family by one."

"We finally got a court date to finalize Shannon's adoption," Kate said. "Next week. Friday afternoon in Judge Wilson's courtroom."

"Next Friday?" Jax asked.

Ben nodded. "We've been waiting for months. This is the first date they had, and we're not sure how much longer we'd have to wait if we don't take it, but…"

"Our wedding rehearsal and the rehearsal dinner," Gwen said.

Kate nodded. "I'm sorry. It's your day, and you two have waited so long for this—"

"And we're not waiting any longer," Jax said.

"Well, there's really no problem, is there?" Gwen said. "It was going to be just family for the rehearsal dinner, and we already have a dinner party planned, anyway. The rehearsal itself is no big thing, right, Ben? We could do that on Thursday or even Friday at lunchtime. We go to Shannon's adoption that afternoon, and then we have the party. We'll just celebrate both things at once."

"You wouldn't mind?" Kate asked.

"No. Not at all. We're all going to be a family. We'll celebrate all sorts of things together over the years, and we'll start now."

"Yes, we will," Jax said, kissing her.

"Unless you think Shannon will feel slighted by not having a party of her own?" Gwen asked.

"No," Kate said, then grinned even wider. "This way we can surprise her with it! We'll be dressed up and together for the rehearsal anyway, and she'll think that's all that's happening. She'd just get nervous about the court date, anyway. She's sure something's going to go wrong, and the adoption won't happen, and I don't want her worrying. I want her to be happy. So we'll just spring it on her that afternoon."

"Good plan," Ben agreed.

"Great plan," Jax said.

"Okay," Kate said. "We're set."

Every now and then, a man had to do certain things that he very much didn't want to do, just to keep the peace. For Joe, lately, that involved agreeing to see his mother. He took her to lunch two days after the wine-soaked picnic incident, as it had come to be known in his mind.

He wasn't used to having so much wine, and he never drank at lunch. That was his backup plan, if he needed one. His main plan was simply to tell his mother to get over it and butt out of his and Kathie's…their…uhhh… He frowned. What to call this thing he was having with her? A relationship? Was it really that? He had no idea.

But he started grinning, just thinking about it.

He was still grinning when he walked into the Corner Diner that day. Heads still turned nearly everywhere when he showed up, but he'd gotten better about ignoring the odd looks, the whispers, the stares. Give him too much wine with lunch and a picnic and a blanket strewn across the grass in an out of the way spot with Kathie, and he could endure most anything.

If it was temporary insanity, so be it. He was ready to embrace it, enjoy it and try not to be too frightened by it.

Then he spotted his mother at a table in the corner with... Who was that?

From the back, he couldn't be sure.

Whispers picked up all around him, and he had a bad feeling about this. A very bad feeling.

"Joe, there you are," his mother said, "Right on time."

That should have been his clue.

Time.

Punctuality.

Winnie!

His mother was sharing a table with Winnie Fitzgerald, a thoroughly disapproving, possibly downright mean-looking Winnie.

"Hello, Mother," he said, ignoring the seat beside her that Winnie patted, wanting him to sit down. "Winnie."

"Joe," she said, in the same way she might spit out the words, *Habitual Truant! School Skipper! Liar!*

"Now, I know you two got off on the wrong foot, but I can't let things end for you like that," his mother said. "Joe, sit down, and let's talk about this."

Fuming, Joe sat, only because he thought he'd

draw even more attention to the three of them if he remained standing. But he wasn't staying.

"I want you to know, I did not put your mother up to this," Winnie said. "She suggested it all on her own."

His mother looked a bit thrown by that. Joe had an idea Winnie was lying through her teeth, but let that go. He had other problems to deal with.

"And I'm not even sure I could agree to go out with you again," Winnie said. "No matter what you might want to say to me today."

Joe thought as openings went, that one was just fine. Plus, it had come up fast, which meant, he could say what he needed to and get out of here, fast. "Winnie, I should have told you before we ever went out that I was seeing someone—"

"You were not," his mother said.

Joe took a breath. "Okay, maybe I wasn't then. I was doing something with her. I honestly couldn't say for sure what it should be called, but I am definitely seeing her now—"

"You are not!" his mother said.

"Yes, I am," Joe insisted. He and Kathie had shared any number of awkward encounters since she'd come back to town, and two meetings that he felt certain most anyone could think constituted dates. He was seeing her every chance he got, and to hell with whether it was smart or not.

"Well!" Winnie said, a pained look on her face.

"Well!" his mother said.

"Neither one of you could possibly be surprised by this," he said. "I'm sure there are new pictures from our picnic, and that you've both seen them."

Winnie gave a snort and looked at his mother, as if to say, *What are you going to do about this?*

"Okay, I'm done here," Joe said, getting to his feet.

"Don't you dare walk out on me," his mother said. "Honestly, I don't know where this incredible lack of manners on your part came from. He's always been the nicest boy," she told Winnie.

"And you've always been a wonderful mother, but I have to say, you've never been more interfering in my entire life," he said, leaning over to whisper it as quietly as possible. "It's time for you to stop. Right now."

Winnie must have heard it, because she gave another snort. "Well, I never," she said. "Are you sure you want to treat me this way? This badly? I mean…there are still people who care about good manners and proper behavior. About telling tales and dishonesty in general."

Joe frowned down at her. "I'm being completely honest with you. I'm seeing someone else, and I really try to only date one woman at a time—"

"And if you'd only done that last year, think what your life would be like right now," his mother said, adding a long-suffering mother sigh.

Joe glared at her. "Okay. I'm scum. Neither one of you should want to have anything to do with me. I think I'll leave now."

He turned to do just that.

"Ooooh," Winnie said, then called after him, "You'll be sorry."

Joe kept right on walking.

Everyone stared. He'd thought he'd gotten used to it, but it seemed he'd thought wrong. This was getting really old.

He stalked out of the restaurant, down the street and back into the bank. Even more stares followed him through the lobby to Marta's office, where he stopped when he realized someone was in his office.

A man, his back turned.

Marta, looking all flustered, hurried toward him.

"Please tell me that's not Jax," Joe whispered urgently.

"No," Marta said, looking like she was terrified. "I'm afraid it's Kate's new husband. And we just got the new glass wall installed."

Joe gave her a dead-on stare. "Kate's new husband is not going to throw me through a wall."

At least, Joe didn't think so.

Although he couldn't imagine why Ben might be here at the bank, either.

"I tried to get rid of him," Marta said. "But he's wearing his clerical collar, and it just didn't seem right, throwing a man of the cloth out of the bank."

"For the last time, I don't want you throwing anyone out of the bank."

"Okay." She nodded, then held up a hand, which was holding her cordless phone. "But I'm ready. I put 9-1-1 on speed-dial after the last time."

"Great," Joe said.

Just great.

He walked into his office. Ben Taylor got to his feet and held out a hand.

"Joe, how are you? Sorry for just dropping by like this without an appointment. Do you have a minute?"

"Sure," Joe said, shaking the man's hand and motioning for him to take his seat once again. He looked over Ben's shoulder to Marta, as if to say, *See? Told you he wasn't going to hurt me.* Joe sat. "What can I do for you?"

"Kate and I need a favor," he said, seeming perfectly comfortable in asking his wife's former fiancé for help.

Okay.

Joe could play that game, too.

"Sure," he said, seeing Marta directly behind Ben, still ready to spring into action with her 9-1-1 call if necessary. "What do you need?"

"You're planning to be at the wedding this weekend?"

Joe fought the urge to make a face. He just loved weddings. The last one he'd attended had been

Ben's wedding to Kate. Kate had asked him person-
ally to come. It had been just after Kate and her
whole family, the whole town even, had found out
he'd been sneaking around with Kathie while
engaged to Kate. In an effort to show there were no
hard feelings between any of them, Kate had
wanted both her sister and Joe there. Joe admired
her for trying, and maybe the talk would have died
down afterward, if Kathie hadn't looked absolutely
miserable during the whole event and left town that
night for six months.

So Joe wasn't really happy about the idea of
going to another wedding.

Especially not a Cassidy family wedding where
the groom-to-be absolutely hated him.

"Kathie wants me to go with her," he said carefully. "And Gwen supposedly wants me there. She
called to make sure I'd gotten the invitation. Jax,
on the other hand—"

"Vow of silence," Ben said. "That's been
working, right?"

"So far," Joe admitted. "But this is his day. His
and Gwen's—"

"It was Gwen's idea to invite you. This is a
family celebration. The whole Cassidy crew is big
on family. You know that, and we're all trying to
smooth things over."

Joe nodded.

"Kate wants her family whole and happy, and I

want that for her. We'd very much like for you to join us both Friday and Saturday. We're finalizing our adoption of Shannon on Friday at 3 p.m. Then we're going to the church for a wedding rehearsal and a christening service for Shannon."

"Oh. Well…congratulations," Joe said.

"Thank you. You'll come?"

"Well…you're really okay with this, too?"

Ben nodded. "I'm a happy man. I want everyone around me to be happy. Especially my wife. Let's put this all behind us, once and for all."

"Well…okay," Joe said, trapped and dreading it. "I'll be there."

"Great." Ben got to his feet, shook Joe's hand once more, then whispered, "Your secretary? I don't mean to pry, but if she needs some kind of help, I counsel people as part of my job. If there's anything I can do…"

"She means well, but she's…different. It's not you. Not really."

"Okay," Ben said. "See you at the courthouse at three."

He left, and Marta came rushing in, breathless and practically yelling.

"Courthouse? You have to go to the courthouse? Are they suing you?"

"No, they're not suing me."

"Because I could be a witness. I'd make a great one. I remember everything, and I often take notes."

Marta frowned. "Why would they send a reverend to tell you they're suing you?"

"They're not suing me," Joe yelled.

Through his newly installed glass wall, he saw more heads turn, seemed to hear his own voice reverberating through the bank.

By nightfall, the whole town would think the Cassidy clan was suing him.

Perfect.

Chapter Twelve

Friday afternoon was chaotic.

Kathie and Kate's bridesmaids' dresses had somehow gotten switched at the dress shop. Kathie had gone home with Kate's dress, and Kate had gone home with Kathie's. Plus, they were all trying to keep the court date to finalize the adoption a surprise from Shannon, hard to do with all the planning for what Shannon thought was only a rehearsal dinner.

Kathie grabbed everything she needed to get ready, plus Kate's dress, and rushed to Kate's to make the switch so they wouldn't have to worry about them the next day. On the way, she called Joe to tell him to pick her up at Kate's. She could have just gotten a ride with her sister, but she and Joe were dating. Surely this was official dating. And she wanted to walk into this family gathering with him. Plus, she didn't want him to have to walk in alone.

"You're sure you're okay with this?" she asked him on her cell phone as she arrived at Kate's.

"I can do it," he claimed, in the same way she imagined most men would claim they could scale a fortress, with grim determination.

"I'm sorry. I know they're a pain sometimes, but they're mostly very nice."

"I know," he said.

Of course, he did. For five years, he'd been part of the family.

But she wasn't going to think about that today. She was going to be happy. She was dating Joe Reed with the full permission, even blessing, of her sister and the promised cooperation of her entire family. Something she thought would never, ever happen, not in her wildest dreams, not in a million years.

"I'm so happy," Kathie said, pulling into Kate's driveway. "We're going to have a good time. Tell me we're going to have a good time, Joe?"

"Well, I know the goal is to have a good time—"

"We're going to have a good time. And I have to go now, because I'm at Kate's. So I'll see you in an hour. Try not to worry." She broke the connection, then tossed her phone into her bag with her makeup and shoes, and off she went.

Kate's house wasn't any calmer. Ben was ready, and he was calm, confirming last-minute details with the restaurant as quietly as possible while Shannon and Kate rushed here and there, borrowing earrings from each other and searching for the right shoes. Kathie still couldn't imagine her ultra-conservatively dressed sister sharing a wardrobe with the former Goth Girl, but apparently, it happened with startling regularity.

"These?" Kate asked, wrapped in a robe standing in the hallway outside Shannon's room, holding up a pair of earrings. "Are these the ones you want?"

"No, the dangly ones. Dangly and blue. I got them last week. I think you wore them to the breast cancer fund-raiser last weekend," Shannon said.

She was in her dress, at least, and her hair was as tame as Kathie had ever seen it, cut into a cute bob that made her look younger than ever.

"Hey, I'm here," Kathie announced, holding up Kate's dress.

"Thank goodness," Kate said, snatching it from her. "Yours is in my bedroom. I was afraid if we didn't switch them tonight, we'd have to ride to church in our bathrobes in the morning."

They all piled into Kate and Ben's bedroom, Shannon searching for earrings, Kate working on her hair and Kathie slipping into the bathroom to tug on her dress for the evening. It wrinkled easily, and she hadn't wanted to put it on until she had to, so she'd just brought it to Kate's.

"Someone zip me," she said when she came out.

"Ohhh, it's tight," Shannon said, zipping her up.

"You think? I didn't think it was too tight." It was a sheath of deep blue with a floral pattern.

Kate sighed. "Tight isn't tight anymore in teen language. Tight is like…good."

"No, really good," Shannon corrected her.

"Oh. Okay." Kathie frowned. "But not too—"

"There's no such thing as too tight," Shannon claimed. "Especially not if you're out to impress a guy. He is coming, right? Your guy?"

"Yes, he's coming." She looked at her sister and positively beamed.

"And you want to impress him, right?" Shannon asked.

"Yes."

"I still have my dog collar necklace. You could borrow it if you want."

"Dog collar?" Kathie repeated.

"Some guys like that stuff," she claimed.

"Joe is not one of those guys," Kate told her.

Shannon giggled. "Hey, you never know."

"I would know," Kate insisted.

"Yeah, I guess you would. And I found earrings, so—"

"Not dog collar ones, right? No dog-collar-like anything today, okay?"

"Nah. It doesn't go with my dress."

Kate gave a long-suffering sigh.

"Sure you want her?" Kathie said. "Because after today, there's no going back."

"I'm sure. I'm just taking the scissors to the dog collar necklace as soon as we get back tonight. Proactive parenting, I believe it's called." Kate smoothed her hair one last time and stepped away from the mirror. "How are you?"

"Nervous," she admitted. "Are we sure this is a good idea?"

Kate shrugged. "We'll be in church. Surely we can behave in church, and the added protection that offers seemed like a good setting for our first real family get-together that includes you and Joe. Yes, I think we'll be fine."

"You're not nervous?" Kathie asked.

"A little," her sister admitted. "But excited and happy, too."

"Me, too." Kathie grinned. It was all she could do to keep from dancing around the room, she was so happy. "I can't believe it's happening. I have a date with Joe. I am dating Joe Reed, and you're okay with that. Kim's okay with it. Gwen's fine, and Jax can't say anything! I never thought this would happen! I didn't think we had one chance in a million of this ever happening."

"Well, it is." Kate fussed with Kathie's hair, tugging on it here, tucking it there and smoothed her dress. "And you look great. Just great."

"It's really going to happen, isn't it? Joe and I, I mean. Everything's going to calm down. People are going to stop staring and gossiping eventually. They'll just get used to me and Joe being together. No more fights. No more emergency room visits. No more black eyes and stitches. It's a real chance for us. For a completely calm, normal, perfectly ordinary relationship. For us!"

"It is," Kate said, giving her a big hug. "And I'm so happy for you both."

Everything was fine at the courthouse. They walked into the courtroom together, and it was just the family. Joe and Jax retreated to neutral corners, doing nothing but nodding at each other, and then the judge gaveled court into session. They all sat. No talking allowed.

Shannon was stunned, moved to tears as first Ben, then Kate took the witness stand, talking about their commitment to each other and to Shannon and what had led them to want her to be a part of their lives forever. Kate cried. Shannon cried. Kathie even cried, sitting close by Joe's side, mopping up her tears with his handkerchief.

She was dating a man who still carried a handkerchief.

It was so very Joe-like, she grinned through her tears.

He slipped an arm around her, comforting and sure, and she leaned into him as they sat there and listened to Kate and Ben, under oath, swear to the strength of their love for each other and make promises about the love and care they intended to provide for Shannon.

It was forever, the judge reminded them, a commitment without end.

They swore they understood, that these were vows they would keep.

Nothing Kathie hadn't heard before, but it was different now, sitting in a solemn court of law, Joe close beside her, her whole family there to witness it. There was no more room for questions about her sister's complete commitment to her new husband and daughter, and it was a beautiful thing to see and hear.

The judge finally proclaimed that from now on, Shannon would be known legally as Shannon Cassidy Taylor, and gaveled the proceeding closed. They broke into applause. There were hugs all around, laughter and more tears.

The scene at Ben's church was every bit as joyous and tearful. They got through the wedding rehearsal quickly, moved on to the christening, performed by the same minister who'd married Ben and Kate, with Jax and Kathie serving as godparents. Then there was nothing but the rehearsal dinner to get through. It was just the family, Gwen's mother hobbling along on her crutches and not looking happy but not saying much to dampen anyone's spirits, plus a few of Jax's buddies from the police force. Kathie thought the cops were glaring at Joe behind her back, but couldn't be sure.

"Almost over," she whispered, as they sat at the long table, Joe between her and Kate, Kim and her date and a beaming Shannon across from them.

Joe gave her a look of mock panic and reached for the glass of champagne that had just been put in front of him. Kathie picked up hers, as well.

"To this being over soon," he said, "without bloodshed or broken glass."

They toasted and drank, the little bubbles feeling funny against her nose and then her throat. "Oh, that's good."

"Yes, it is."

An attentive waiter helpfully topped off their glasses without being asked.

Kathie wasn't much of a drinker, but the official toasting began, and they had a lot to toast—a wedding, an adoption, the family being together, the beginning of new lives together.

Before she knew it, she was a little tipsy.

She'd been too distracted and too nervous to eat much, and the waiter was much more proficient at keeping the champagne glasses full than the water glasses, and she was thirsty. So she had some more champagne. By the time the dancing started, and she got to her feet—none too steadily—to dance with Joe, she thought she might have a problem.

He laughed and invited, "Okay, just hang on to me."

And then, she was in his arms, the music dreamy and slow, the lights on the restaurant's tiny dance floor turned down low.

This was another moment she'd dreamed of all her life.

The two of them easing around a cozy, dimly lit dance floor.

He was a wonderful dancer, so solid to hang on to and sure of himself. They started out in a perfectly respectable embrace. Kathie just closed her eyes and let him lead her around the floor. But the music was soft, sexy jazz, made for smoky back rooms and snuggling, and it was like his body kept calling to her.

Closer.
Come closer.
Closer still.

She eased ever closer. It was like those first kisses when she came back to town, the ones in the alley where time seemed to stand still, and he'd been caught, unable to move more than a breath away from her. When he just had to kiss her. Every now and then her thighs brushed against his. Then she could feel the muscles in his chest and his abs. She rubbed the tip of her nose against his neck and his jawline.

His breath warmed her ear as he whispered, "I think you've had a little too much champagne."

"I think I haven't had enough of the champagne or you."

Closer still.

There was a nice little kick of heat simmering between them. She wanted to start a fire.

He groaned and pulled her hard against him. In the dark, in a corner of the dance floor, his mouth found hers, and she gave hers eagerly, hungrily to him, until her head was spinning in the best of all possible ways.

It was the best night of her life, she decided.

This was heaven.

There was no other word for it.

Heaven.

Joe wasn't clear on much that happened after they started necking on the dance floor. He knew the party was breaking up. He knew as they stepped outside the restaurant, one of Jax's friends from the police force pulled opened the door of a waiting cab and said, "I think this is a good idea tonight."

Okay.

No arguing with a cop. Especially not a friend of Jax's.

He probably shouldn't drive. He wasn't much of a drinker, but the champagne had gone down way too easily that evening. Probably because the whole night had felt like him being thrown into a pack of wolves, with Jax and three of his best cop friends there.

So, yes, he'd had a bit too much to drink.

But the cab was fine. They could both sit in the darkened back seat, and no one had to pay attention to the road. Which meant, he had Kathie in his arms again, as he had on the dance floor.

He remembered the driver asking for his address and giving it automatically, not really thinking about anything but kissing Kathie some more. He'd been a bit puzzled when they'd arrived at his house instead of her apartment, but not sorry.

Neither was she.

They barely made it inside before they were kissing again.

All he'd really wanted was to be able to kiss her with no one around. Kiss her maybe sprawled out on his couch with his hands all over her, where no one could see. Where no one was armed with a cell phone with a camera.

She'd looked so pretty and so happy tonight.

Beautiful, even.

He didn't remember ever seeing her so happy, seeing her smile so much and seem so free. The Kathie he knew was quiet and had a bit of reserve.

She was shy and sweet, and while those things definitely still applied, there was a sexiness about her that was killing him.

The little blue dress she wore was decidedly short, showing off her legs to perfection and the curve of her hips and her breasts. The material was shiny and silky, sliding over all her curves every time she moved, making him want to have his hands all over her, too, and the moment they were alone, that's what he did.

He had his hands all over her.

He had her pressed up against his closed front door, his body trapping and holding her there, his hands gathering up her dress until he found bare skin on her thighs, up over her hips, then slid down inside lacy panties to cup her hips and pull her to him.

Oh, this was bad.

So bad.

She lifted one leg and hooked it around his waist, sending the thought of nothing but not-so-innocent kisses right out of his head.

He scooped her up into his arms and deposited her on the couch, tugging off the jacket of his suit and his tie. She took care of the buttons of his shirt, and her dress was up around her waist, giving him a view of really gorgeous legs and little sky blue panties that were almost all lace.

Oh, that was not fair.

Not fair at all.

His head was spinning in what seemed to be a very good way, but he'd been taught that there were certain ways a man treated a lady and devouring her on his couch while they were both half-drunk on what might generously be considered a third date was not one of them.

Especially not someone like her.

A good girl.

She sat up, blinking at him curiously like she might be seeing three of him or something, or might just be trying to figure out what was wrong.

He sank down to his knees on the floor in front of her, which brought him way too close to those pretty bare thighs.

She smiled at him, and her hands went to work on the buttons of his shirt.

"Kathie, honey, we need to think about this."

"I've thought about it long enough," she said. "For years, I've been thinking about this."

Which was exactly why he needed to be very careful with her.

He'd built a life based on being careful, calculating every risk and planning his moves, one by one.

Kathie on his couch in blue lace panties, undressing him, was a big, big risk to take, and he'd never quite calculated his next move with her from here.

His hands fell to her thighs, by accident really, then slid back and forth along the length of them, knees to hips.

She looked at him like a siren and took his mouth with hers.

Kissing her was like a drug he'd never, ever tried, highly potent and definitely illegal.

"I can't think straight when you do that," he complained.

"Why are you thinking at a time like this, Joe?"

Yeah, why was he?

Because that's who he was, the kind of guy who'd try to fight off the sensation of warm, smooth skin beneath his hands, pretty thighs spread out on either side of him, her arms entwined around him, holding him close.

It's Kathie, he told himself.

This is Kathie Cassidy, and she should be treated like spun glass.

Except she was like a wildfire in his arms.

Even the finest of glass melted under the right kind of heat, after all.

They generated serious heat.

His whole body was throbbing. He buried his mouth against the side of her neck, her delectable neck, obviously quite sensitive from the way she started squirming beneath him, both trying to get away and trying to get closer at the same time. He palmed her breasts through the dress, and then his mouth left wet circles on the material as he tried to get to them through the fabric. He should have taken off the dress, but it was easier, faster to just push it up, bra and all.

There.

Bare breasts in his hands, his mouth all over them, her writhing beneath him.

Time slowed, finally, the frenzy easing just a bit.

She made the most delicious sounds as he teased her pretty curves.

"Perfect," he told her. "You're perfect."

His mouth trailed down her rib cage on one side, tickled at her side. She squirmed away from him again, and he ended up with his mouth on her right hip bone, which gave him all sorts of other ideas.

Like the fact that those little blue panties needed to come off.

He slid his hands beneath them on either side and tugged. They snagged on something, gave and came down those perfect thighs, and he was nuzzling her with his nose, making his way up those same perfect legs. She froze for a long moment, not objecting, not doing anything, and then started to shiver. Which made him want her even more.

"Let me," he said, his mouth moving low on her belly.

"Joe—"

"Trust me," he said.

And then she didn't do anything but moan.

He palmed her hips once again, scooted her out to the edge of the cushion and buried his head in her waist, devouring her in a whole new way.

She came in seconds, literally, and he kept going, wanting more, kept going until she begged him to stop because she was exhausted and couldn't take it anymore.

Things moved in a frenzy from there. He ripped off his clothes and his shoes. He sat down on the couch beside her, took her limp body in his arms and sat her on his lap, facing him, her dress scrunched up around her neck, arms around his neck, face pressed against his shoulder, her pretty thighs on either side of his.

A moment to adjust their positions, and then, there they were, heat to blessed, liquid heat. He held her hips in each of his hands and eased her down ever so slowly.

"Like that," he murmured to her, kissing her cheek. "Just like that."

Her thighs tensed against him, her hips. He held her gently, guiding, showing her the way, whispering to her, wanting nothing but to be buried inside of her, while she slowly, slowly sheathed him.

"I don't know if this is going to work," she said.

"It's working," he told her. "Working very well, right this minute."

Slowly enough to drive him insane, but it was

working. He palmed her hips, moving her into a little rocking motion, fighting with everything he had the urge to thrust up inside of her and finally be where he had to be.

She groaned, her entire body plastered against his, holding on so tight, like she might fall to pieces if she let go.

"Kathie, you're killing me. Let me in."

Then her body gave way, and there he was, in one smooth stroke, deep inside, surrounded by her.

Yes, that's what he wanted. What he craved.

Her.

She went limp again in his arms, draping her body over his, boneless, putting herself completely in his arms.

"Okay. I've got you," he promised, rocking her body ever so slowly up and back against his, thinking if they went at this slowly, easily, he might be able to make it last.

She groaned and shuddered against him. It went on and on and on, until she sank her teeth into his shoulder to keep from crying out.

How he made it through that, he'd never understand, but he did it, he made it, then got the exquisite pleasure of easing her back on the couch and following her down.

He wasn't done with her yet.

Chapter Thirteen

Kate was getting ready for the wedding the next morning when her doorbell rang. She answered it to find Kim, who was looking for Kathie.

"She's not here," Kate said.

"What do you mean, she's not here? Her car's here."

"Because she drove over here with my bridesmaid's dress yesterday and decided to get dressed here for the rehearsal dinner, because we were running out of time. Joe picked her up from here."

"Oh." Kim looked worried.

"She didn't come home last night?"

"I don't think so. I mean, I'm not sure. She hasn't been there this morning, at least not since I got up.

And it's not like her to just disappear and not tell me anything."

"She wasn't home when you went to bed?" Kate tried.

"No, but I wasn't worried. I mean, she left with Joe. What's going to happen to her with Joe? I mean…" Kim grew silent. "You don't think…I mean, even if they were…you know… she wouldn't spend the night at his place, right? They'd pretend they weren't. She wouldn't want pictures of her leaving his house, wearing her dress from last night, making the rounds."

No, she wouldn't.

Ben came into the living room and immediately said, "What's wrong?"

"Kathie didn't come home last night."

"Oh."

"One of us has to go find her," Kim said.

"We do?" Ben asked, looking hopeful that the answer was no, that they didn't have to go find her.

"Did you try her cell phone?" Kate asked.

"Of course. She didn't answer."

"Let me try." Kate picked up the phone and dialed, then could swear she heard the faint ringing of a phone in her own house that didn't belong to her or Ben or Shannon. "Do you hear that?"

"Yeah. The back bedroom, I think." Ben headed down the hallway and into their third bedroom, coming back with a ringing phone. "No Kathie, but she left a bag of stuff yesterday, when she got dressed here. The phone was in it."

"Okay." Kate groaned. "She doesn't have her phone, but she left the restaurant with Joe? Did anyone see them leave?"

"I saw them heading for the door together," Ben said. "Kate, we went through a lot of champagne last night. You don't think something happened, do you?"

"Joe is the most responsible man in the world. He wouldn't drive if he'd had too much to drink."

"He most definitely had too much to drink. They both did, but they didn't drive," Shannon announced, walking sleepily down the hall in her pajamas and heading for the kitchen, yawning as she went.

"You know this for certain?" Ben asked.

She opened the refrigerator and stuck her head inside. "Yeah. I saw them get in a cab together outside the restaurant. Why? Are they lost?"

"Something like that," Kate said.

Shannon laughed and stuck her head up out of the refrigerator. "You mean, someone didn't come home last night?"

"Something like that," Kim said.

"You're not going to tell me to go into the other room, are you?" Shannon asked. "I mean…I've had a baby and given her up for adoption already. I don't think there's anything you can say that could surprise me or shock me."

"Well, they're probably fine," Kim said. "I mean, if they took a taxi somewhere together, they're fine, right?"

"But the wedding's in less than two hours. We're supposed to be at the church in forty minutes," Kate said. "Have you tried calling Joe's?"

Kim nodded. "It rings busy, over and over again. It's either out of order or someone took it off the hook, which I guess could be a clue."

"Try Joe's cell?"

"No."

"Okay," Kate said. "I will. I can do this."

She grabbed a phone and dialed, with no idea of what she might say if he answered. But no, he didn't.

"It went straight to voice mail. His phone's off."

"I told everybody in the church to turn their cell phones off last night before we started the rehearsal," Ben said. "I always do that. I bet he never turned his back on."

Kate closed her eyes and groaned. "One of us has to go find Kathie."

They all just looked at each other, Kim standing there with her hair going every which way, Ben unshaven and in jeans and a T-shirt, Shannon in her pajamas. Kate was afraid she was the closest one to being ready, having already showered and dried her hair.

"I'm not going," Kim said.

"Me, either," Ben said.

"Well, I don't want to go," Kate said. "What if they're…you know!"

"Oh, we're in weird territory here," Shannon said. "I'm getting in the shower. I can't go anyway. I don't have a driver's license or a car."

She disappeared down the hallway.

Kate wanted to cry. "Okay, let's review. If we don't find her, and she doesn't make it to the church in time for the wedding, Jax will stop the ceremony himself and organize a search party. Believe me, Jax is the last person Kathie would want to find her or that we would want to find her and Joe that way. If they're really…that way."

"Right." Kim agreed. "You're the oldest sister. You have to go find her."

"She'll be so embarrassed. I'll be embarrassed," Kate complained.

"But you won't knock Joe through a wall," Ben said.

"Oh, fine," Kate said. "Way to stick up for me."

"I'll go if you really want me to," he said. "I'm just thinking if she is there with him and they're…in some potentially embarrassing situation…she'd rather have you find her than me."

"You're right," Kate admitted. "Now that I think about it, it's probably more important to have you keeping track of Jax. He really doesn't need to know anything about this. It's his wedding day. He should be happy."

"Okay. I'm on Jax patrol."

"And I could go to Gwen's. Quickly. Just to make sure Kathie's not there, and I'll call you," Kim said. "If she's not there, you'll know you have to go to Joe's. There. We have a plan."

Kate frowned.

She hated the plan.

Kathie was snuggled deeply inside what had to be the warmest blanket on earth, half-asleep and never wanting to wake up when her blanket moved beneath her.

That was odd, she thought in a warm, fuzzy, thoroughly distracted way.

She went to burrow farther down into it, hoping to sink deeper into sleep, a vaguely uneasy feeling telling her she really didn't want to wake up, when the blanket gave a soft groan.

Odd.

She could have sworn a moment later, her blanket sounded just like Joe and that he was saying her sister's name.

Kathie jerked upright, blinking in confusion, coming awake in Joe's living room, on Joe's couch, with what seemed to be Joe's naked body stretched out beside her.

"Ahhh!" she said, jumping off of him and taking the blanket with her.

"Ahhh!" he said, looking up at her, seemingly as confused as she was.

She was at Joe's, naked.

He was naked.

They'd…they'd…

"Oh, my God!"

"Oh, God!" he groaned.

Then she remembered she could swear she'd heard him say her sister's name.

"You called me Kate!" She was furious. And hurt. Furious and hurt. She was going to kill him. "Of all the things I ever imagined you saying to me in a moment like this, my sister's name is the absolutely last one—"

"I didn't call you Kate. I was answering Kate." He looked completely baffled as he grabbed his pants from the floor and pulled them on. "I could swear I heard your sister's voice."

"So I sound like her?"

"No, you don't sound like her."

"Tell me I'm not a substitute for her, Joe. Tell me."

"Kathie, no. Listen to me. I'm telling you I think I really heard her voice. Like she was here."

And then, there it was. That was her sister's voice, calling out Joe's name. Someone was knocking on the door.

"Did we lock that?" Joe asked. "Because I'm not sure I did."

"I don't know. You didn't lock it?"

They turned toward the door in horror.

It started to open.

Kathie groaned, picked up her blanket and ran for the bathroom down the hall, praying as hard as she could that this was a nightmare. That the whole thing was a nightmare.

She locked herself in the bathroom, tucked the blanket more securely around her and then splashed cold water on her face, one, two, three times. Then dried her face and stared at herself in the mirror.

She was at Joe's.

It was morning.

She felt a little fuzzy-headed from what had no doubt been too much champagne.

And she'd spent the night with Joe.

Oh, and just for added fun, her sister was here for some reason.

This could not possibly be real. It was some kind of guilt-induced dream, remnants of how awful she felt about kissing Joe last year while he was still engaged to Kate, no doubt brought on by the fact that she seemed to have done much more than kiss Joe last night.

That had to be it.

She sank back against the locked door, her legs hardly enough to hold her up momentarily, and then she went and sat down on the edge of the tub.

The world seemed to be a very, very strange place this morning.

She thought back through exactly what she knew. First, she felt certain it was morning. There was no clock in the bathroom, but there'd been daylight coming in through the windows, she believed.

Joe's windows.

Joe's house.

Joe's couch.

Joe's naked body stretched out on the couch and wrapped around hers.

Kathie closed her eyes and buried her face in her trembling hands.

She and Joe…in this crazy, delicious frenzy of want and need…it had been nothing like she imagined her first time would be. She grinned in spite of the situation in which she found herself.

It had been so much more.

Deliciously more.

Wickedly more.

Exhilaratingly more.

"Kathie?" Joe's voice came to her tentatively from the other side of the door. "Kate's here."

Kathie wished she had X-ray vision so she could see through the door without opening it, without either one of them being able to see her. "Why?"

"Well…it's nine-forty in the morning. You're supposed to be at the church in twenty minutes for the wedding, and no one could find you. When they'd looked absolutely every place else, Kate came here."

"Oh," Kathie said. "Okay."

As potential disasters went, she supposed this wasn't so horrible. It could have been her brother who'd found her this way.

"She's going to wait outside in her car, in case you want her to drive you to the church or her house or yours or anywhere you want to go."

"Oh. Okay."

She could take her pick. A ride from Joe or one from her sister? Which would it be in this most awkward of moments?

"I have your clothes, if you need them," he offered.

Kathie unlocked the door, opened it no more than six inches and cowardly stuck nothing but her hand out, took the clothes without so much as touching him, then locked the door once more.

Okay.

She couldn't stand the idea of getting dressed in last night's clothes and opening up that door right now. And she had a family wedding to think about.

Shower? She could do that in three minutes flat, if she really hurried. Yes, she needed a shower.

"Tell Kate I'll be out in five minutes," she said.

Don't think. Shower, she told herself.

Shower. Dress. Wedding. Act like nothing happened. Deal with this later.

That was her plan.

It was a good plan.

Except Joe's shower, his soap, his shampoo, everything in here, smelled like Joe. Once she got out, she'd smell just like Joe, which would make it even harder not to think about him and what had happened and how she felt about it, how he might feel about it and what might happen between them now.

All not things she really wanted to be thinking about or dealing with in front of her whole family at her brother's wedding.

Okay.

No helping that.

Because she'd gotten tipsy at the rehearsal dinner and slept with Joe. Or maybe he'd gotten drunk and slept with her. She'd have slept with him drunk or sober, but she couldn't be sure if he'd have done the same.

Although—not that she really had any experience to judge by—he certainly had seemed like he wanted her last night. Had to have her, was more like it. Was ready to devour her, actually, which made her blush from head to toe, just thinking about it.

Running her own soapy hands over her own naked body, even as fast as she could in her frantic shower, was bringing back all sorts of memories. His hands and his mouth, the sound of his voice, the way he moved inside of her, the way it felt to have him there.

She groaned again, shampooed and rinsed her hair in record time, then climbed out of the shower and looked down at her rumpled dress with distaste.

"Joe?" she called out tentatively. "My dress for the wedding is in your car. Could you get it?"

"I'm afraid my car's at the restaurant," he said. "Remember?"

"Oh. Yeah."

"Want a pair of sweats and a T-shirt? I got them for you, while you were in the shower, and a bag to put your clothes from last night in."

"Oh. Okay."

How thoughtful, she decided.

He was a very thoughtful, well-organized man.

Or was it just…experience in having unexpected guests spend the night and not want to go home in the clothes they'd worn over there?

Kathie didn't want to think about that.

She unlocked the door, took the clothes from him and tugged them on, wrapped her hair in a towel, shoved the clothes she'd worn the day before into his gym bag and she was ready. Nothing left to do but face him and her sister.

She turned to the door and leaned her forehead against it for a moment, fighting the urge to bang her head against it instead. Joe was right on the other side of the door, and her sister was outside.

Her entire family was probably at the church waiting or soon would be. Was this some bizarre form of punishment after all, even if Kate had all but handed her Joe on a silver platter?

"Kathie? Are you okay?" he asked.

She flung open the door, stood in the doorway, trying not to analyze in a thousand different ways, every little nuance of his expression, the tone of his voice, the look in his eyes.

"We don't have time to figure this out now," she said. "Besides, I don't really know how I feel about it. Do you know how you feel about it?"

"No," he said.

"Good. Me, either. Which means there's no reason to talk anyway, because we have no idea what we'd say. So I think we should just put this off until after the wedding. Okay?"

"Okay?" He seemed to be asking if that was the right answer, looking like he desperately wanted to get this answer right.

It was sweet, and silly, and so totally Joe that Kathie stood on her tiptoes and gave him a big kiss.

"But...it was good." She grinned like crazy. "Really, really good. And not at all like I imagined it would be."

"Good?" He nodded. "Okay."

She touched a little, reddish-looking bruise on his shoulder. "I think I bit you there. Sorry. I was trying not to scream."

Then she blushed like crazy, grabbed her shoes and ran out the door, hoping none of his neighbors saw her. Kate was indeed waiting in her car in the driveway, making a really funny attempt at looking like nothing out of the ordinary had happened.

Of course, she would do that. That was Kate.

Kathie threw the gym bag with her wadded-up dress in the backseat and climbed into the front, and there was the bag she'd left at Kate's yesterday, with makeup and her blow-dryer and most everything she'd need to get dressed for the wedding.

"Oh, thank you," Kathie said when she saw it. "Thank you, thank you, thank you."

"You're welcome," Kate said.

"We have to go get my dress. It's in Joe's car, which is at the restaurant."

"Okay. We can do that."

Kate put the car in reverse and was backing out of the driveway when Joe came rushing out the front door and toward them.

"Keys," he said, holding them out to Kathie when she rolled down her window. "You'll need keys to get into the car."

"Oh. Right. Thanks."

He looked from one of them to the other, the expression on his face saying he'd just as soon eat worms than have to face them both this morning.

"Want a ride to your car, Joe?" Kate asked politely, staring straight ahead.

"No. No, thank you," he said, when surely inside, he was saying something more like, *No way in hell am I getting in the car with the two of you to go anywhere this morning.*

"See you at the church," Kathie said, and they were off. They'd been traveling for a full minute before she added, "Okay, I'm really sorry about that. That was… I mean, it was bad enough before when…" She and Joe hadn't done anything, but now that they had… "I never thought about this part."

That she'd slept with Joe, and that over the course of a five-year engagement, she'd bet her sister had also slept with Joe. Now they'd both slept with Joe.

"Let's not think about it," Kate said.

"Okay. Let's not."

Except, it was impossible not to think about it.

"But, you're okay?" Kate asked.

"Of course. I love him." All the awkwardness in the world couldn't overcome that one simple fact. She loved the man, and now she'd spent the night with him. She looked to see how that was going over with her sister.

"Good," Kate said. "That you love him, I mean, and that you're happy. That's what matters. That you love him, and you're happy. I'm happy for you."

"Thank you."

Which couldn't help but lead her to thinking that not everyone would be happy about this.

"So, how bad is this? That you had to come looking for me, I mean?"

"Well, Kim knows you didn't come home last night, and when she couldn't get you on your cell phone, which was in the bag you left at my house, she came over to see if you were there. Where she talked to me and Ben and Shannon…sorry about that. Shannon walked in, in the middle of it. But she's the one who knew you and Joe left the restaurant in a cab, so we didn't have to worry you'd gotten into an accident or something."

"Okay." That was good. Calling the hospitals looking for both of them would have been bad, calling the cops, even worse.

"Kim went to Gwen's and managed to find out you weren't there without giving too much away, and I sent Ben to babysit Jax to try to keep him from finding out anything about… anything."

"Good. Oh, that's so good," Kathie said.

So if they could just get through the wedding and the reception without Jax finding out and getting upset, maybe throwing a punch, they'd be okay.

"Thank you," Kathie said again.

"So, we'll get your dress from Joe's car, and then…go straight to the church? If we go straight there, we might beat everyone else there, and then no one else would wonder why you're wearing Joe's clothes this morning."

"Okay. We can do that," Kathie said.

"Is there anything…you want to talk about?" Kate asked. "Anything you need?"

"Oh…underwear," she said, a pained expression on her face. "I need underwear to wear under my dress. I don't want to go to my brother's wedding in yesterday's underwear. I can't. And I really don't want to call Kim and ask her to bring me some. And I don't want to have to go into a store and buy underwear while I'm wearing Joe's clothes or a bridesmaid's dress with no underwear on."

The underwear was about to be her undoing.

"We'll wash them out in the sink in the bathroom at church, and I'll dry them with your blow-dryer while you're doing your makeup," Kate said.

"I can't do that." Kathie tried silently begging her sister, *Don't ask why. Please don't ask why.*

But Kate said, "Why?"

Kathie groaned and hid her face in her hands.

"Couldn't find them?" Kate asked, then burst out laughing.

"No. I found them. And we weren't going to talk about this, remember?"

"I know, but… You mean…your underwear? It doesn't exactly…work anymore?"

"No. Don't! Don't ask me. Don't make me tell you."

"Are you telling me that Joe Reed…" Kate broke off into giggles again. "One of the most polite and careful men in the world ripped your underwear off of you last night?"

"Yes. Okay? Yes. That's what happened."

When she finally gave up hiding her face and her flaming cheeks and looked over at her sister, Kate was grinning wickedly.

"Good for you," Kate said. "And for him."

And it was wrong. It was absolutely wrong, and she'd sworn to herself that she would never, ever do this, but she was dying to know, so she said, "He was really…polite with you?"

Kate giggled and nodded. "I was, too, but I'm not anymore, and…we really shouldn't talk about this."

"You're right. We won't. I'll call Kim. I'll ask her to bring me underwear." If she could get through the conversation she'd just had with Kate, she could ask Kim anything.

Chapter Fourteen

Joe did indeed have what looked like a bite mark on his shoulder.

He leaned closer to his bathroom mirror, turning this way and that, trying to get a better look, because...well, because he didn't think a woman had ever left a mark on him before.

Another first in the life of Joe Reed.

Now that he thought of the mark, while he'd been talking to Kate and trying not to look at her, and she'd been trying just as hard not to look at him, he did think he'd caught her giving him a really odd look, but not in the face.

In the shoulder?

Yeah, maybe that had been what the odd look was about.

He leaned over the bathroom sink, splashing cold water on his face again and again and again, thinking that if he ever told this story to any other guy, they'd tell him he should put it in one of those fantasy letters to *Playboy. Bedding the Cassidy Sisters, by Joe Reed.* Not that he'd ever write one of those or tell anyone about this.

He dunked his whole head under the stream of water in his sink trying to get the idea of what he'd done out of his head.

It was so un-Joe-like.

His life was completely un-Joe-like at the moment. When he straightened up again and looked in the mirror, he still couldn't quite believe what he was seeing.

He'd had too much champagne and had sex, none-too-gently he might add, with Kathie Cassidy on his living room couch and woken up to find his ex-fiancé outside his door looking for her sister because Kathie was in danger of being late for their brother's wedding.

Okay, if he thought of the all-time worst thing that could have happened, he supposed they could have actually slept through what was supposed to be the beginning of her brother's wedding, and her brother could have found them naked on Joe's couch.

So this morning wasn't the absolute worst.

Although seeing Kate this morning, at his house, in the same room where he'd just had sex with Kathie, with Kathie naked in the bathroom...well, that had been bad.

At least no one had pictures.

Unless someone had snapped one of Kathie leaving his house this morning. Would anyone believe they'd had sex last night, and her sister had picked her up from here this morning? Joe didn't think so, so they were probably safe on that score.

And there was no way he was going to that wedding today.

No way.

He'd had enough Cassidy family gatherings for one weekend.

He turned on the shower and stepped inside, one highly disturbing image of Kathie being in here, stark naked, not ten minutes ago, not doing anything to help him forget all the things he should be forgetting this morning.

Her naked, his hands all over her, the way she wrapped her arms around him and draped her body over his, letting him do whatever he wanted to do with her, like she trusted him completely. He didn't think he'd done anything to deserve that kind of trust from her, something that would normally be a given with him and a woman.

She'd just been so sweet, a little shy, and yet eager to touch him, to explore, to get so close to him t was impossible to tell where he left off and she began.

He hadn't even gotten her dress off of her the first time.

Not until the second time, when he had her spread out on the couch beneath him, had he taken the time to tug her dress and her bra completely off of her and let himself sink down into her eager arms and her warm, welcoming body.

And the way it had felt to be inside of her, with…

With…

Joe just had a very, very bad thought.

Him, inside of her, with absolutely nothing in between them?

Like…no condom?

He didn't keep condoms in his living room, because he didn't normally have sex on his couch. When he had sex with a woman, he wanted to be comfortable, almost always on a nice, big, comfortable bed. So back in the days when he'd kept condoms in stock, they'd been in the nightstand by his bed.

And he knew he hadn't ever made it into his bedroom last night, which meant…no condoms.

Joe turned to the tile wall of his shower and bashed his head none too gently against the wall again and again.

He hadn't needed a condom in years, because he hadn't been with anyone since he broke up with

Kathie's sister six months ago, and before that, he and Kate had been together for five years. He'd trusted her, and she'd trusted him, and over the course of five years…well, they'd dispensed with the condoms a long time ago. Joe wasn't even sure if he still had any in the house, but if he had, they'd be in his nightstand, and he hadn't gone near it the night before.

And he really, really didn't want to have this discussion with Kathie Cassidy, but he didn't see that he had any choice.

He wasn't waiting to have the conversation, either.

Which meant, he had to go to the damned wedding after all.

He dressed in a rush, nicking his jaw while shaving, and he seemed to have left a reddish bruise on his forehead from bashing it against the shower wall. At least the bite mark on his shoulder was covered by his shirt and jacket.

All he had to do was get inside the church and grab Kathie for a moment and talk to her, then get out.

That was it.

He wasn't staying. This was not going to become a big, public thing, like everything else had become.

He grabbed his keys, his wallet and his cell

phone, which was off, probably since he'd been in church the night before for the wedding rehearsal. He turned it on as he headed for his car.

Which wasn't there.

It was at the restaurant.

Lucky for him, one of his neighbors, Andrea Ross, worked with Gwen at the local floral shop and was leaving for the wedding at the same time Joe walked by. She offered Joe a ride, giving him a few odd looks over his less-than-perfect appearance, but thankfully didn't ask any questions.

"Forgot to turn on my phone last night," he said, when they were in the car and moving. "I just need to check my messages."

"Sure, Joe. Go ahead," Andrea said.

He had messages.

He hit a button and heard his boss's voice. *Need to talk to you right away. Call my cell.*

Joe frowned.

He had a bad feeling about this.

Was it the fight? He'd thought they'd gotten past that. Not that it was forgotten, just that it could be overlooked as a temporary aberration, given how long Joe had been with the company without any even remotely similar incidents. But maybe not.

Maybe life was about to get worse than he thought.

Bob Welsh answered on the first ring, a clipped, abrupt, "Welsh here."

"Bob, it's Joe Reed. Sorry I didn't get back to you last night. I had my cell off."

"Joe." Heavy sigh. Not good. "What has happened to you?"

"I'm really not sure, sir."

"Me, either, son. Me, either. I thought when we talked after the incident at the bank that you understood. You came about as close as someone can come to being fired without actually being fired."

"Yes, sir."

"And then I hear that you're in restaurants in your town getting into fights over women. Wine is being thrown around in public. You're leaving public restaurants soaked in alcohol?"

Winnie? He knew about him and Winnie?

Joe thought about saying, *One woman. Only one woman and one glass of wine.* He couldn't bang his head against the car because he wasn't in his car or alone. He was in his neighbor Andrea's car, and she was already looking at him funny.

"And then, I hear you're taking sick days so you can partake in a drunken picnic in the middle of a town park on a work day?" his boss said.

"I wasn't drunk, and I haven't taken a sick day in years," he said.

More furtive glances from Andrea as she drove. A little faster, or was that Joe's imagination? Was she scared of him now?

"I know you haven't taken a sick day," his boss

said. "And I really don't mind one every now and then. But you really don't want to spend a sick day drunk in the middle of the day, in a public place, where all your employees can parade by or at least hear all about it, Joe. What were you thinking?"

"I guess...I wasn't," he said.

"You have to. You have to think what kind of example that sets for the people who work for you. Do you have a drinking problem, son?"

This morning, he most decidedly did.

"Sir, I—"

"Because you sound like you had a rough night."

Joe started laughing, couldn't help it. It had been a disastrous night. He wasn't even sure how bad yet. And he was sure, Andrea looked scared now.

"Tell you what we're going to do," his boss said. "I'm suspending you for sixty days, and we'll find you a nice clinic somewhere that can help you with your substance abuse problem—"

"I do not have a substance abuse problem," he insisted.

"I saw the pictures, Joe—"

"There are pictures?"

"Lots of pictures," Andrea whispered to him.

"Of you at the park with red wine and a woman all over you," his boss said. "I'm sorry. It's a suspension and treatment, or I'm going to have to fire you."

"You're kidding?"

"No, I'm not," his boss said. "What's it going to be? The clinic or you're done with us?"

Joe bit back six different kinds of swearwords, virtually all he knew. He felt like his head was about to explode.

Careful, he cautioned himself. *This is your career. Years of your life. How you earn your living. Pay your bills. Fund your retirement account.*

Retirement?

He didn't think he was going to live that long.

He had no more patience, no more reasonableness left in him, and he just couldn't think straight anymore. Surely last night had proven that.

"Fine," he said. "I'm done."

His boss was still talking when Joe hung up on him.

"Bad day?" Andrea asked very, very tentatively.

"Yes. A very bad day."

"Well…surely it will get better. We're here."

He looked out the window and there, in the parking lot, sat what looked like nearly every cop car in town, Jax's cop friends, here for Jax's wedding.

Great.

He thanked Andrea for the ride, wondered if she'd heard the part where he'd gotten fired, if that news would make the rounds during the wedding.

By the time he got into the church, most everyone else was already there. He kept asking people where the bride was, thinking the brides-maids had to be with the bride, but apparently they were locked away somewhere from prying eyes. He must have looked a little unsettled this morning, because people seemed uneasy around him.

It didn't help that the church was indeed filled with cops, all of whom would rather hit Joe than look at him.

One of the biggest, burliest-looking ones came up to Joe and said, "We don't want any trouble today, now do we?"

"No, we don't," Joe said. "No trouble. Not today."

He took a seat at the very back of the church and shut up, wondering if it would be really bad to try to catch Kathie as the bridesmaids lined up in the vestibule before marching down the aisle.

Okay, that would probably be bad.

He sat there drumming his fingers on the wooden pew in which he sat, glancing furtively behind him every few moments, looking for Kathie. It seemed like every time he looked back, there was another cop friend of Jax's glaring at him from somewhere in the church.

They were everywhere.

He drummed his fingers some more.

If they only knew what kind of trouble had already found him the night before....

Kathie.

It always came back to her.

The thing was, he just didn't think Kathie Cassidy was the kind of woman who made a habit of bedding men. Knowing her the way he did, he was almost certain it would be something she very rarely did. And women who did that sort of thing very rarely weren't the kind of women who would make regular use of some method of birth control, and if that was true, then…

Joe started to sweat, right there in church.

Had he been so crazy for her that he hadn't taken the most basic of precautions? Shown the least shred of responsibility?

He fought the urge to bang his forehead against the back of the pew in front of him, then looked over to see two women who looked only vaguely familiar giving him an odd look.

"What?" he asked.

"You seem a little nervous," the one said.

Joe nodded. No use denying it when it was painfully obvious.

"I thought you had a thing for Jax's sisters?" her friend asked.

"I do. Did. I mean, I did have a thing for the one, and now I have…a thing for the other one."

"But not his fiancée, right?"

"Huh?" Joe said.

"You just like the sisters?"

"Only two out of the three," Joe said, as if there were some virtue in that.

"Okay. Just wanted to make sure you didn't have a thing for Gwen, too. That you weren't going to make trouble here."

Another sad commentary on his current life. That people would be scared to have him in church for a wedding, scared he'd not only go after two of the groom's three sisters, but the bride as well.

Joe gave them as reassuring a look as he could manage. "Never laid a hand on Gwen. Promise."

"Good," they said.

"Let me guess. You ladies are married to some of Jax's friends on the police force, right?"

They nodded.

Great.

He had a feeling he'd be trailed by cops everywhere he went at the reception. How would he ever get a moment alone with Kathie in which to ask, *Excuse me, and I'm sorry. I know this is rotten of me, but…please tell me we didn't have sex without any form of birth control last night. Please.*

How would he get to say that with any sort of privacy?

While he was waiting for the wedding party to finish with the photographs and make it to the reception, Joe got to wait and think.

He was trying to figure out if either he or Kathie might have said anything about precautions of any kind, which meant going over in as much detail as he could remember, everything that had happened the night before.

Which wasn't doing anything for his ability to think clearly. He kept getting way too caught up in details of an erotic and explicit nature.

Even facing disaster, Kathie did this to him.

Her and that silky dress he'd found so easy to slide up her thighs and those little blue panties that had been almost completely lace. A wide band of pretty lace wrapped around her slim hips.

He remembered fighting to get them off of her. He might have actually torn them in the end.

Torn lace panties…

Should a man apologize for something like that?

Certain men, he knew, would simply be proud, but did a man like him, a polite, normally careful man apologize?

What would Miss Manners say about this?

She probably didn't address it in any of her publications, Joe decided, leaning against the wall, hiding out in a corner of the room, waiting for Kathie.

Cops were everywhere, circling and glaring.

He tried to look as nonthreatening as possible. A few of them had stared at his forehead, maybe thinking he'd been in a fight already this morning, because he'd banged his own head into a wall?

Joe tried to smile and forget about torn panties.

And the body that had been inside of them.

He tugged on his tie, which was growing too tight by the moment, and took the barest sip of his drink, more champagne, not a good omen, he feared.

Had Kathie been drunk?

Had he taken advantage of a woman while she was drunk? Had he sunk so low? And was it taking advantage if she'd come to him so willingly and eagerly?

He had been tipsy at least. A little past tipsy, but he didn't have the excuse of being drunk out of his mind. He'd just been uneasy about going into the family gathering, then relieved to think he was going to make it through without any major blowups, hadn't eaten much and had drunk more than he should have.

He thought she was only tipsy, too. Or a little past tipsy.

How bad was it if she was a little past tipsy?

Again, Miss Manners would be no help, he was sure.

There was rudeness. There was bad behavior. There was irresponsibility. There were unplanned pregnancies.

Onto which part of the scale did his behavior fall?

"You look like you're about to be taken out and shot," Shannon said, sneaking up beside him when he wasn't paying any attention.

She looked completely different from the girl Kate had taken into her home last fall, looked like a girl, a normal, happy teenage girl. She'd been in the wedding party and was here, which meant Kathie should be here soon.

"Is there some plan you know about that I don't?" Joe asked.

"No, but if Jax finds out Kathie didn't come home last night, and that she was with you..."

"We really don't want him to find that out today, now do we?"

"I guess there's been enough bloodshed between the two of you. And it is a wedding." Shannon stood there grinning, like she had nothing better to do than torment him.

"Thank you. How considerate of you."

"Oh, wait. I forgot—did Kim remember to tell you about Ms. Fitzgerald?"

"Winnie?" Joe said.

"Yes. Kim heard at school from a teacher, who got into a fight with Ms. Fitzgerald for not reporting kids being late to class when we really are, that Ms. Fitzgerald's been saying people are going to learn not to mess with her."

"Believe me, I'm not going to be messing with her," Joe said.

"Kim's friend said that Ms. Fitzgerald said her godfather is some big shot bank executive in Atlanta, and that he's your boss."

"Bob Welsh is Winnie's godfather?"

"I don't know his name," Shannon said. "But, I guess that would be bad, huh?"

"Yeah. Bad."

"You should have asked me before you took her out. I could have told you how scary she is."

"I wish I had," Joe said.

"So, you were just mean to Ms. Fitzgerald because she was mean to you, right? You're going to be good to Kathie? I mean, you'd better be, or else," she said, sounding like a full-fledged member of the Cassidy clan, which she officially was as of yesterday.

"Believe me, I've been warned," he said.

A year and a half ago, no one would have thought they needed to warn him of anything like this. No one would have expected him to be anything but good to a woman and careful and responsible.

And look at him now, desperately needing to know if he might have just impregnated his former fiancée's sister.

She finally arrived. Joe made a beeline for her, but so did everyone else. She knew practically everyone in the room, and they all were curious about her and Joe. They were nearly as popular as the bride and groom.

Joe shook hands, kissed women's cheeks and stayed by Kathie's side, acting as he imagined a dutiful, well-mannered escort would, one who hadn't ripped anyone's panties off and forgotten his condom.

Kathie, at his side, absolutely glowed, her arm slipped through the crook of his, a delicate hand with pink-tipped nails resting on his forearm.

He was trying not to think of that hand on his chest, clutching at his shoulders, running over his body, the way she smelled or the warmth of her beside him.

Or her naked.

He really didn't need to think of her naked.

They were forced to sit down to a late lunch. After the meal, after they toasted the bride and groom, and then had done every other wedding thing he could imagine, he got her, somewhat alone, in a corner of the room.

"Hi," she said, beaming up at him, looking a little shy, a little uncertain, but very, very happy. "How are you?"

"Okay," he lied.

"You cut yourself shaving." She touched a hand to his jaw.

Joe nodded.

He really liked those hands of hers on him.

He was starting to sweat, he feared.

"And did you hit your head?" She touched him there, too.

"I was banging my head against a wall this morning," he said, then wished he hadn't.

She laughed. "Why? I mean...I know it wasn't

the best morning after we might have had, and granted, I don't have a lot of experience with things like that, but…last night…Joe, it was wonderful."

He nodded.

She looked worried. "You mean…it wasn't?"

"No. I didn't meant that—"

"You were disappointed?"

"No," he insisted.

"I did something wrong?"

"No—"

"Because I've never really…you know."

He stopped short at that. "Never really…"

"You know…" she said.

"No, I'm not sure I do, and this would be a point on which we should be absolutely clear." More importantly, before he'd ravaged her on his couch—that would have been the time to be absolutely clear about this. But he hadn't done that, either.

"So, you couldn't tell…that I'd never…done that before?"

Had wild sex on a couch with a man who ripped your clothes off? Most of them, at least?

He couldn't bring himself to say it, and he feared he already knew the answer. She had been so sweet and eager, but shy, too, and hesitant, uncertain. Innocent, he feared.

As in…completely, virginally innocent?

"You'd never been with a man before?" he managed to get out.

She shook her head, looking a little embarrassed, but pleased with herself, as well. "I just...I always wanted it to be you."

Kill me now, Joe thought. *Just kill me now.*

"Did I hurt you?" he whispered urgently. Because that was his first concern.

"No. It was a little...uncomfortable, but just for a moment, and then it was wonderful. Really. And I thought you liked it, too."

"I did. Way too much."

She laughed, her hand toying with the lapel of his jacket. "How can you like it too much? I mean, you're supposed to really, really like it, right?"

He groaned, took her by the arms and tugged her farther into the corner with him, not wanting anyone to see them. "Kathie, I was a little...no, we both had a little too much to drink last night."

"Yes."

"And I'm not saying I didn't want it to happen, because I did. Very much. But I don't want to think I took advantage of you in any way."

"Don't be silly," she said. "I wanted you, too. I want you again. As soon as Jax and Gwen leave—"

"No. Wait. Just...wait." Not again. No way were they doing this again until they'd cleared this up. How to even approach the subject? "Look, I haven't been with anyone else in a long time."

Other than her sister, which they were not going to talk about.

"I mean...I haven't had to worry about any sort of precautions, and granted, it's a lousy excuse. It's no excuse at all. There is none. I just...I didn't use a condom last night. I'm sorry. I didn't, and unless you were using something..." He trailed off, waited.

Her eyes got really big and round, scared-looking, and that told him everything he needed to know.

He turned his head and swore softly and at length, then made himself face her again. "I'm sorry. Like I said, there's no excuse. I don't know what I was thinking. I just...wasn't thinking."

Her mouth fell open, but it was a while before she got out any words. "I guess I wasn't thinking, either. I didn't expect it to happen so quickly with us."

"I know."

"And when it did...I had trouble thinking of anything at all, except that...it was happening, and I was so happy and I wanted to do everything right and...I guess I thought you'd take care of every-thing."

He nodded gravely. He should have.

"And I know that's not fair," Kathie said. "Not fair at all. I just...I've never had to worry about anything like that before. Oh, Joe. I feel so stupid."

"Me, too," he said.

"And I was so happy." One single tear slowly rolled down her cheek.

He felt like a complete jerk. Like an idiot. "Kathie, please don't."

He went to pull her into his arms and comfort her, but someone stepped between them, putting his back firmly to Joe, so that he couldn't even see Kathie anymore. One of the guys who'd been glaring at him for most of the wedding, one of Jax's friends no doubt.

"Kathie, honey, is he bothering you?" the guy said.

"No," she said, her tears falling faster.

"Because I know who he is, and I'd be happy to get him to leave you alone."

"No. It's okay."

Joe thought the guy growled in his direction, but he couldn't be sure. He didn't know a lot of guys who growled.

God, what a nightmare.

The guy settled for one long, hard look at Joe and then stepped away, all of maybe five feet. Obviously, he was still considering taking action.

"This is crazy," Joe said, dropping his voice to a whisper again. "It's crazy."

"I'm sorry," Kathie said, again and again, he felt like an absolute jerk.

"I don't want you to be sorry. I don't want—"

"What? Me? You don't want me?" she cried.

"That's not what I said—"

"Because you sure seemed like you did last night.

Not that I have much to judge it by, but it sure seemed like you were completely into me last night, Joe."

"I was, all right? I was. The thing is, every time I touch you, some disaster happens. Surely you see that?"

"No," she protested.

"It does. I get within ten feet of you lately, and it's complete and utter disaster. My life is falling apart all around me. I've been thrown through a glass wall in my bank by your brother."

"I'm sorry about that."

"My boss was ready to fire me for that, and you'd think I would have learned something from it, walking around with a black eye and stitches for a week, but no, that wasn't enough. For months, everyone in town has known I was sneaking around behind your sister's back with you, and that was bad enough, but I just couldn't stay away. I couldn't do it."

"I couldn't either. I couldn't stay away from you—"

"People are throwing drinks at me in public places. Winnie was so mad, she got her hands on a picture of us at our picnic and e-mailed it to my boss, who happens to be her godfather, who was not amused. He thinks I have a substance abuse problem and wanted me suspended and in rehab for sixty days—"

"Joe, you're yelling—"

"And when I refused this morning, he fired me. I don't even have a job anymore. My own mother thinks I've gone nuts, that I'm about to turn into my no-good, irresponsible father—"

"No, you're not anything like him."

"I just can't think straight around you. I can't think at all. It's like you've short-circuited my brain or something. I take you to bed with me...oh, hell, we never even made it to the bed. I don't even bother to find out that you've never been with a man before, and now I may have gotten you pregnant."

He finally fell silent, and only then realized there was a great deal of silence left when he stopped speaking.

Like, maybe there weren't a whole lot of other people in the room talking, either. Like, there might have been more people listening to him than talking.

Which was a bad thing.

A very bad thing.

With a growing sense of dread, he looked down at Kathie, who stood defiantly before him, tears rolling down her cheeks but her head held high as she made it through every word he'd said, taking it like the punishment he'd never intended it to be.

Then he dared look around them to see cops gathered in a half circle, standing between him and Kathie, and what seemed to be a growing crowd. Kathie's sisters were the only people who'd been allowed in the inner circle, and they both looked horrified.

Okay, this was bad.

Joe turned back to Kathie, who hadn't moved a muscle, an expression of shock and anger frozen on her face.

"I'm sorry," he said. "It's not you. It's me. There's just something wrong with me when I'm with you, and…I'm sorry, Kathie. Really, I am."

At which point, the cops closed in on him.

"What do you want us to do with him, Kate?" one of them asked.

"Just hold on to him for a minute until Jax leaves," she said. "And then we'll figure something out."

Fine, Joe thought, deciding he deserved everything he was about to get.

Kathie watched them take him away.

She knew Kate and Kim were at either side of her and was grateful for their support. Kate found a tissue and started mopping up Kathie's tears.

"Listen to me," Kate said. "Gwen and Jax are leaving. You are going to stand behind Kim and me, so Jax doesn't get a good look at you, while we wave and try to smile and send them off on their honeymoon, okay? And then, we'll figure out what to do, just the three of us."

"Okay," Kathie said. The last thing she wanted to do was ruin her brother's day.

His perfectly happy day, with a woman who loved him and whose life didn't turn to disaster when she got near him.

She followed her sisters to the front of the church hall, hid behind them and waved when they told her to wave.

Gwen turned at the last minute and hurled her bouquet straight toward Kathie's nose. The only thing that made her catch it was not wanting to get hit squarely in the face with it.

The minute the car carrying the bride and groom disappeared around the corner, she stalked back inside the church, walked right up to Joe, a cop holding him by each of his arms and hurled the bouquet in his face.

Then she ran out the side door of the church hall, around the corner and behind a tree. A moment later, she found herself in her two sisters' loving embrace.

"I was so happy," she said. "I've spent my whole life waiting for him. Ever since I first saw him, I thought he was everything a man was supposed to be. I've measured every man I've ever met against him, and no one ever came close."

"I know, honey," Kate said.

"I thought he was mine now, finally, that he loved me the way I love him," she cried. "And I was just so happy."

Chapter Fifteen

It was three weeks later before Joe figured out what to do, and another week after that before he found the nerve to do it.

He stopped as he got off the interstate about fifteen miles from town, at a little strip shopping center that had a drug store. He prowled the aisles—lost—turning down help from an ultra-attentive clerk twice before he found the section he was looking for.

Home pregnancy tests.

She would know already, wouldn't she?

But if she didn't, the last thing she'd want to do in Magnolia Falls was buy a pregnancy test. The news would spread like wildfire.

Assuming that no one had been gossiping already about the little chat he and Kathie had before he skipped town right after the wedding. Granted, that was a huge assumption. But just in case, he figured the least he could do was buy the pregnancy test for her here, where no one knew either of them.

He was trying to be a gentleman for a change, be considerate, not the jerk who'd yelled at her at her brother's wedding and made her cry, then disappeared for a month. Honestly, he was surprised Jax hadn't sent a posse after him by now.

Joe frowned as he inspected the incredible variety of home pregnancy tests. Single test pack or double? He sure didn't plan to be in this position more than once. He'd go for the single.

Test strip?

Test cup?

Color change?

Word change?

What the hell?

He grabbed three and went to pay for them, thinking surely that would cover all the bases.

He put them down on the counter, and the clerk gave him a really odd look.

"What? Men don't buy these?"

"Not usually, no."

Joe looked behind the clerk, just so he wouldn't have to look the woman in the eye, and his gaze landed squarely on row upon row of condoms.

Which had him thinking…if the test came out a certain way, and the things he had to say to Kathie came out a certain way, and he was very, very fortunate at some point in the near future, they might have need of the condoms.

"You know, I think I need a pack of those, too." He pointed in the general direction.

The clerk turned around, grabbed what turned out to be a colossal box and held them up to Joe. "These?"

Joe nodded. If he was going to be hopeful, might as well be very hopeful.

"And three pregnancy tests?"

He nodded one again. "People don't usually buy them both at the same time?"

"Not usually," the woman said.

He handed over the money, took his bag of merchandise and left, the little restaurant on the corner noting that it had a bar, also, calling his name.

One, he told himself. Just one.

Buying the pregnancy tests had taken a lot out of him.

He walked into the restaurant, dark and quiet, just what he wanted, and found a seat at the bar, the pregnancy tests and condoms in a bag on the empty stool beside him. Ordering a drink, sipping it slowly, he tried a bit longer to delay the inevitable, facing her, saying what he had to say and waiting to hear her answer.

"Hey," a guy in a baseball cap and worn jeans three stools down said. "Don't I know you?"

Joe glanced over, thinking, *Maybe,* but what he said was, "Don't think so."

"Yeah, I do. You from Magnolia Falls?"

"Maybe," Joe said, because if Kathie wouldn't take him back, he was probably leaving town for good.

"Yeah, I know who you are. My niece works at the high school in Magnolia Falls. Some bigshot school administrator. Been dating this hotshot banker until he dumped her."

"You've got to be kidding me," Joe said, because he'd so hoped his life was about to take a turn for the better. He was turning it around completely. Starting today.

"Yeah. Winnie Fitzgerald. Sweet girl." The guy got up off of his stool and took a menacing step toward Joe. "I think you know her."

"Look, Winnie and I—"

"Son, I gotta tell you. I have a hard time believing you're a guy who managed to do two sisters at the same time," the guy said, laughing like it was the funniest thing he'd ever heard.

That did it.

Joe stood up and knocked him to the floor with one punch.

Yeah, life was getting better.

* * *

Jax got the radio call just as he was going off-duty, and he tried to turn it down, but a buddy of his in dispatch said, "Trust me, you want to handle this yourself. Bar fight, out at Kelly's by the interstate. I'm not going to say what the bartender said started it, not on the radio. It would just make you even madder."

Okay.

He called Gwen on his cell phone to say he was going to be late. It was July 4, and his family was gathering in the park for a cookout and to watch fireworks. Then he hightailed it out to the bar.

His blood pressure started to rise when he saw a certain gray late-model sedan in the parking lot, especially when he got a look at the plates.

Yeah, he knew that car.

So, the rat was back in town, drinking and fighting to boot.

Jax couldn't wait to get his hands on the man.

He strode into the bar, finding not a fight but a mouthy guy in one corner with a busted lip. In the other was Joe Reed, with a bruised cheekbone and bleeding from a cut on his lip. The bartender, a guy Jax knew from his high school football team, was standing between them, trying to keep the peace.

"There! Finally," the mouthy guy yelled. "'Bout time. I wanna press charges. This idiot walked in here and attacked me."

He pointed at Joe, who looked at Jax and murmured, "Wouldn't you know it? You're on duty, huh?"

Jax nodded to the bartender, Adam Green, to let him know he'd handle things from here. Then he made a fist with his right hand and started flexing his muscles to warm them up. He didn't care if it did get him suspended. He didn't care if it got him fired. This was his little sister they were talking about, and a man didn't do something like this to his little sister without paying for it.

"I should have kicked your butt last year when I had the chance. And about a dozen times in between," Jax said.

"Take your turn," Joe invited. "No problem."

"Wait," mouthy guy asked. "You're not gonna arrest him?"

"How about I beat the crap out of him, and then I'll arrest him. We'll say you did it, but that he started it. How about that?"

"He did start it," the guy said.

"Right. I knew you'd back me up." Jax was going to enjoy this.

"Wait," the bartender stepped between Jax and Joe. "I don't know if you want to do that. You haven't heard the whole story."

"Believe me, I want to hit him," Jax said.

"Don't think you do," Adam insisted. "Joe was provoked."

"I don't care." Jax laughed.

"You will. I bet you won't be arresting anybody—"

"Whadda you mean, he won't be arresting anybody?" mouthy guy said. "This guy went nuts and started hitting me. That's assault. And all I said was that he didn't look like the kind of guy who'd be doing two sisters at once."

Jax froze. He saw red, then wheeled around to face mouthy guy. "What did you say?"

"I told you not to say that again," Joe said.

"Why? It's true, isn't it?"

Jax grabbed the guy by his shirt collar and nearly hoisted him off the floor. "The thing you need to know, first, is that it's none of your damned business."

"Hey, take your hands off me—" The guy started squirming, not that it would do him any good. Jax was a whole head taller.

"Second, it's not nice to talk about a lady like that. Or two ladies, in this case."

"I just—"

"And third, the ladies in question just happen to be my sisters!"

"Oh, hell," the guy said, cowering and trying to cover his face.

Jax dropped him to the ground with a thud, and it took every bit of self-control he had not to do something worse.

"That's what this was about?" he asked the bartender.

"That was it."

"Did they mess up the bar or anything? You want to press charges?"

"No, I'm good. Just get 'em out of here," the bartender said.

Jax stood over the guy he'd just dropped to the floor. "Joe, you want me to arrest this guy for starting a fight with you?"

"No, I'm good," Joe said.

"Arrest me?" mouthy guy complained.

"Yeah, that's what I'd do. And you've got to know, you don't want to be alone in the back of a police car with me today. I don't think it would be safe. There's no telling what I might do to you between here and the jail, especially with that mouth you've got on you."

The guy started mumbling about not needing to go anywhere, and that his mouth did tend to get him into trouble, that maybe he should learn to keep it shut.

"Good. That's good. We're done here," Jax said, grabbing Joe by the arm. "And you're coming with me."

"Hey, wait. Joe? I think this is yours." the bartender said.

Jax turned around to see his friend shoving three home pregnancy tests and a humongous box of condoms into a bag and holding them out to Joe.

Joe took them, looking like he was thinking about what to order for his last meal.

Jax said, "It's a damned miracle I don't kill you right here. You know that, don't you?"

Joe nodded.

"But first, you're going to go see my sister—"

"That's where I was headed," Joe claimed, as Jax shoved him through the door and outside.

"Sure you were. And just to make sure, I'm taking you to her myself."

"My car is right there. I was heading back to town—"

"I'm driving," Jax said, and then, just because he could, slapped a pair of handcuffs on Joe and shoved him into the back of the police cruiser.

A month to the day since Joe Reed flipped out at her brother's wedding and disappeared, there hadn't been one single scandal big enough to take the place of that little scene as the hottest gossip in town.

Kathie had prayed for scandal, almost as much as she'd prayed that she wouldn't turn out to be pregnant, and still, no one had done anything remotely gossip-worthy.

Which meant, as she walked through the park on July 4 that it seemed every eye in the place was following her.

She made it past a group of older women, head

held high, until she got a glance at one who looked like Joe's mother.

Oh, please. Don't let it be Joe's mother!

The only possible worse thing that could happen would be running into Winnie Fitzgerald, who was still mad, even after she'd gotten her godfather to fire Joe.

Kathie kept walking, head averted so that if it was Joe's mother, she might not recognize Kathie. She finally made it to a shady spot on the banks of the river near the falls, where her family—minus Jax but plus the dogs, Romeo and Petunia—had gathered. Ben had hamburgers sizzling on the grill. Shannon was dancing to what was no doubt some really obnoxious music being piped straight into her ears, and her sisters and Gwen were huddled together looking worried.

Kathie forced a fake smile across her face. She wasn't the first woman to be disappointed in love, and she wouldn't be the last. She wasn't the first to be absolutely devastated, she was sure, it just felt like it at times.

Because she'd loved him.

Loved him completely and hopelessly for years, and couldn't it have just stayed that way? In the realm of the hopeless? Rather than moving into possibilities and then reality and finally sheer disaster?

She didn't understand that part.

Couldn't she just have never had a real chance with him? Was that too much to ask?

Getting closer, she saw that Gwen was on the phone, her sisters huddled around her, hanging on to every word she said. Kathie went and greeted the dogs, who were sprawled out on the grass, sunning themselves.

The minute Gwen put her phone away, Kathie said, "What's wrong now?"

"Oh, honey," Kate said. "Brace yourself, all right?"

Oh, God. "What?"

"Jax found Joe," Gwen announced.

Kathie took a step back, landing with her back against a nearby tree. "Found him? What does that mean, he found him?"

"I'm not exactly sure," Gwen said, looking a tad uneasy. "But…it's good that he found him, right?"

"I don't know," Kathie said. After a solid month of thinking that any moment, he would turn up, that he would come see her or call her and say he was sorry or at least tell her what he planned to do, she wasn't sure if she was ready to know. She was terrified of what he was going to say.

Kathie leaned against the tree, then slid down to the ground, her legs unable to hold her up any longer.

Her sisters sprang into action, Kate by her side, holding her up, as if she might fall over into a dead faint at any moment. Kim ran to get some water and brought it to her. Gwen fanned her with a pot holder she'd grabbed off a hot dish on the picnic table.

"Oh, geez. I'm not going to pass out," she said miserably, feeling not just their eyes, but every eye in the park within seeing or hearing distancce, on her once again. She might cry, but she wasn't going to pass out.

Then she looked up and saw her brother striding down the middle of the main walkway in the park toward her, dragging Joe along with him.

Joe with his face unshaven, bruised and with a bloodied lip, a disreputable-looking T-shirt untucked, a ratty pair of jeans that absolutely molded to his legs and hips like nothing she'd ever seen him in before, and…

"So…what do you think?" Kathie heard one of her sister's ask Gwen.

"I'm thinking…I never thought I'd see Joe Reed look this way. What are you thinking?"

"That I'm surprised Jax hasn't killed him," Kim said.

Kathie laughed, a scary sound. "I keep thinking about that silly song they sing in the fairytale. Sommmme-Daaay Mmmmy Prinnnccce Will Commme…. But, I never thought it would be like this. If he's even coming here for me."

"Wait. What's that on his wrists?" Kate asked.

"I don't know," Gwen said.

Oh, God.

"Is he handcuffed?"

Romeo, a former police dog, gave a big woof and trotted off toward the two men, ready to guard the Cassidy sisters from any and all troublemakers.

"Yeah, I think you're right," Gwen said. "He is handcuffed."

Kathie buried her face in her hands. She couldn't look. Just couldn't.

And she'd thought things couldn't get any worse?

"Hello, ladies," her brother said. "Look who I found in the middle of a bar fight on the edge of town."

"In a bar fight?" Kate asked.

"Yeah," Jax said. "Make some room."

Kathie looked up as her sisters backed up, and her brother shoved Joe none too gently toward her. Still handcuffed, he landed mostly sitting up under the tree facing her.

Romeo gave Joe a menacing look, then started sniffing him.

"Back off, Romeo," Jax ordered, and Romeo did, but he didn't go far. He was a good dog.

"Jax, you're not making this any easier by arresting him," Kate said.

"I didn't arrest him. I had a chance to, but I didn't. And you don't want to know why. It would only upset you. But all I did was bring him back here. I'm damned well going to make sure he apologizes to my little sister."

"Go away," Kathie yelled.

"You want me to get rid of him?" Jax asked. "Because if that's what you want, I'll get rid of him. You don't ever have to see him again—"

"No, I want you and everybody to go away," Kathie said. "It's bad enough that everybody at your wedding heard our last argument. I'd like to have this one in private. Although this spot will just have to do, because I'm not going anywhere with him."

"Okay, if that's what you want. Everybody, back up," Jax said. He herded them all, including the dogs, away, and then, just before he left Kathie alone with Joe, he threw a plastic shopping bag on the ground at Joe's feet. "I'm guessing he bought these for you, Kathie."

She opened up the bag, because she thought that would be better than having to look at Joe or anyone else for a moment. Then realized the bag contained three home pregnancy tests and the biggest box of condoms she'd ever seen.

"Ahhhh!" she yelled again. "You're going to find out if I'm pregnant, and then make sure you never impregnate anyone else?"

"No. I just didn't want you to have to buy them in town," Joe said. "The tests, I mean. If you haven't already bought one."

"If you're going to ask me if I'm pregnant, Joe, at least have the guts to come right out and ask me."

"I'm not asking," he said. "I don't want to know."

That brought her head up, her eyes locked on his. "You don't even want to know?"

"No. That's not what I meant. I want to know. But not yet. Don't tell me yet. Let me say what I need to say first, okay? Because I don't want you to ever think I said this because you might be pregnant. That's not why I'm saying it, Kathie. Please believe me about that, okay?"

She wanted to. Oh, God, she wanted to.

And it was impossible not to see that he looked like he'd been in worse shape than she had been in the past month. His hair was longer than she'd ever seen it—granted, not really long for anyone else, but long for Joe—actually brushing his collar and falling almost into his eyes. It was fuller than she realized and thick. The bruise on his cheek and the little cut at the corner of his lip only added to the badboy look.

It was…well, kind of sexy. Rough, but sexy.

"Oh, God." She groaned, and buried her face once again.

"What? I didn't even say anything yet."

"Okay, just say it and get it over with." She didn't have to look at him. Not if she didn't want to.

"I'm sorry," he said.

"Me, too. News flash. We're both sorry. Anything else, Joe?"

"I missed you."

"Oh, right?" she yelled, head back up, glaring at him.

"I did. It was incredibly…quiet without you around."

"Boring, you mean. That's what you want, isn't it? A nice, safe, sane life?"

"No. I want a life with you," he said.

She groaned yet again.

"Okay, that didn't come out right. I have to back up. I never should have said those things I did to you at the wedding. It was awful. I was rude and mean and all of these things I never wanted to be, especially not to you. You're…you're wonderful and sweet and so…" He stopped to take a breath. "I don't know, Kathie. Everything. My life, when I'm with you, is completely different than I ever thought it would be, and that scared me at first. Okay, worse, it was terrifying. I'm sorry about that. But after a while…I liked it—"

"You did not!"

"No, you're right. I loved it, Kathie. I didn't quite see it until it was gone, and I'd left. I spent weeks trying to figure out how to put my old life back together again, the one I had before anything happened between us, and then I realized, I didn't want my old life back. I didn't want anything I thought I wanted before. I just want you."

"You cannot possibly mean that," she said.

"I do. I mean it. I swear it."

"You just think I'm pregnant, that's all. And if I'm pregnant, this is what you have to do, because it's the right thing to do, and you always try to do the right thing."

"Okay, at first, I did think you were pregnant, and I was thinking about the right thing to do, but then…it was the funniest thing. The more I thought about having to come back here and marry you, the happier I got. Because there was no decision to be made then, just what I had to do. And it turned out, what I thought I had to do was what I absolutely wanted to do. I just had trouble admitting it to myself at first."

"I don't believe you for a minute," Kathie said.

"It's true. If you were pregnant, I could just come back and marry you. There was no trying to get my nice, sane, predictable, incredibly boring life back. It was gone for good. I'd get to be with you. It's like saying I was going to jump off a cliff—"

"You think marrying me sounds as appealing as jumping off a cliff?"

"As exciting as jumping off a cliff. As surprising. As freeing. I don't want to be that guy I've always been. That careful, list-making, wearing-his-shirts-according-to-a-rotation-plan, working-at-the-bank dull guy."

"You're not dull. Not at all—"

"I want this crazy thing you do to me. I want to feel the way I do when I'm with you. I want to not care about what anybody thinks, and play hooky from work—once I find another job—and drink wine off of you at picnics in the park in the middle of the day. I want to laugh and be happy and strip you naked on the couch and just about everywhere else I can think of. I want that life. Please tell me that's what you want, too?"

Kathie was crying then. "Joe…I'm not pregnant, okay?"

His expression didn't change, not one iota. "Okay. Would you like to be?"

"You don't mean that."

"Well." He shrugged as best he could, considering he was still handcuffed. "Maybe not right away. It would be nice to have some time to ourselves first, I guess, but eventually, don't you want to have kids? Because I do."

"I'm saying, you don't have to say any of this—"

"I do. I have been miserable without you. I've missed you like crazy."

"I'm not even sure you like me—"

"Kathie, honey, it's so much more than that. Anything that feels this strong, this out of control, this crazy…I think it has to be love."

She fell silent at that, hope finally taking root and starting to grow. "I didn't think you could ever love me."

"What can I say? It takes me a while, longer than it should have to figure things out. Especially with you, and I'm sorry for that. But one thing about me—I generally get things right in the end. I'm in love with you."

She blinked up at him, finding it hard to move, hard to say anything else.

"Unless, you don't want me like this," he said, looking honestly worried. "I mean, maybe you want the boring, predictable guy. Ahhh, damn, I didn't even think of that. Is that who you want, Kathie?"

"He's the one I always thought I wanted," she admitted. "I always thought I'd be so safe with him, because he seemed so strong and like he had absolutely everything under control. I thought he could handle anything."

"You never thought he'd be sitting in front of you in handcuffs, jobless, lucky he hadn't been arrested, bringing you a home pregnancy test?"

"No, I never thought that about him."

"Is that what you want, Kathie. Do you want him?"

"Oh, Joe. Did you mean what you said? You really missed me? You were happy thinking you had to come back here and marry me?"

"Happy doesn't begin to cover it. I was thrilled. I broke laws to get here. I was going ninety miles an hour, with the windows down and the wind in my hair, singing at the top of my lungs along with the radio. I'm talking that kind of happy. Kathie, I know

I'm no prize, sitting here like this with my life all messed up, but…if you don't want me anymore, tell me."

"No. I…it's the craziest thing," she said, shaking her head. "This new you. This out of control, impulsive, punch-throwing guy." She smiled through her tears. "I like him even better."

He froze. "Really?"

"Well, I could do without the bar fights—"

"Hey, I have one thing to say in my own defense. Winnie Fitzgerald. Winnie is everywhere—"

"You did not get into a fight with Winnie." He'd never hit a woman.

"No. Her uncle. First person I ran into when I came back to town. The next was your brother."

"Sorry about that. At least you didn't end up in the emergency room this time. I'd rather not have to track you down in the emergency room and be scared that you'd really been hurt."

"I think I could stay out of the E.R. from now on. And I'll find another job. I've got some money in the bank. It's not like we'd be destitute."

"I'm not happy that your mother thinks I'm something akin to the plague—"

"Or that your brother wants to kill me, but we can work those things out, can't we?"

He finally made a move toward her, leaning down to kiss her softly on her mouth, lingering there, touching her so sweetly, then making her think of the night she'd spent with him, that wickedly satisfying night that she'd been sure was going to be one of the greatest disasters of her life.

"I have to tell you something first," she said, wishing her brother had taken those stupid handcuffs off, so she could have felt his arms around her. She'd really like to have his arms around her right now. "I actually don't know if I'm pregnant or not. I haven't taken the test. I didn't want to know. I was afraid you'd come back and ask me if I was, and I didn't want to be able to tell you. I wanted you to make up your mind about me. Just me."

"So…you think you are?"

"I don't know. My life has been kind of a mess, and my body is… I don't know. Not normal, but that could just be me worrying and feeling sick to my stomach because I didn't know if you were ever coming back—"

"Kathie, honey. You had to know I'd come back." He leaned over and kissed her again.

"I thought you would, but a month is a long time, and I did kind of tear your life apart. I'm really sorry about your job at the bank—"

"I'm not. I'm sick of the bank."

"Who knew Winnie Fitzgerald had connections like those?" Kathie started to laugh.

"Who knew?" Joe said. "Guess it's a good thing I bought the pregnancy tests, but I'm not giving them to you until you say you'll marry me."

"Joe, are you sure?"

"I'm sure. And I wanted to do this right." He shifted his weight, propped himself up on his hand-cuffed hands and managed to get up on one knee. "Kathie Cassidy, will you marry me?"

Kathie eased up onto her knees, pressing her body against his, intending to kiss him soundly, but first, "Okay, I guess I should tell you, we probably don't need the tests. I'm actually pretty sure I am. Pregnant, I mean."

She watched him absorb that, unblinking, a slight grin raising the corner of his mouth where it had been cut by someone's fist. He didn't look upset. He looked like a man who could handle anything, which was one of the first things she'd loved about him.

"Okay," he said. "Answer the question. Are you going to marry me? And it had better not just be because I got you pregnant."

"It's not," she said, leaning in for that kiss.

But she was a little off balance, or maybe he was. They ended up pitching sideways onto the grass, laughing as they went and kissing, Kathie doing her best to hold on to him since he couldn't hold on to her.

"I bought a ring," he said. "It's in my pocket, and I can't quite get to it right now. But I have a ring to give to you. I want to give you everything."

"I want to give you everything, too, and I want to see my ring. Jax!" she yelled as they lay on the grass. "Get these handcuffs off the man. I'm going to marry him."

* * * * *

New York Times *bestselling author*
Linda Lael Miller
is back with a new romance featuring
the heartwarming McKettrick family
from Silhouette Special Edition.

SIERRA'S HOMECOMING
by Linda Lael Miller

On sale December 2006,
wherever books are sold.

Turn the page for a sneak preview!

Soft, smoky music poured into the room.

The next thing she knew, Sierra was in Travis's arms, close against that chest she'd admired earlier, and they were slow dancing.

Why didn't she pull away?

"Relax," he said. His breath was warm in her hair.

She giggled, more nervous than amused. What was the matter with her? She was attracted to Travis, had been from the first, and he was clearly attracted to her. They were both adults. Why not enjoy a little slow dancing in a ranch-house kitchen?

Because slow dancing led to other things. She

took a step back and felt the counter flush against her lower back. Travis naturally came with her, since they were holding hands and he had one arm around her waist.

Simple physics.

Then he kissed her.

Physics again—this time, not so simple.

"Yikes," she said, when their mouths parted.

He grinned. "Nobody's ever said that after I kissed them."

She felt the heat and substance of his body pressed against hers. "It's going to happen, isn't it?" she heard herself whisper.

"Yep," Travis answered.

"But not tonight," Sierra said on a sigh.

"Probably not," Travis agreed.

"When, then?"

He chuckled, gave her a slow, nibbling kiss. "Tomorrow morning," he said. "After you drop Liam off at school."

"Isn't that…a little…soon?"

"Not soon enough," Travis answered, his voice husky. "Not nearly soon enough."

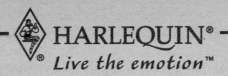

HARLEQUIN®

Live the emotion™

American ROMANCE®

Heart, Home & Happiness

⟡ HARLEQUIN®

Blaze™

⟡ Harlequin® Historical
Historical Romantic Adventure!

Red-hot reads.

⟡ HARLEQUIN®

HARLEQUIN ROMANCE®
From the Heart, For the Heart

⟡ HARLEQUIN®

INTRIGUE

Breathtaking Romantic Suspense

Medical Romance™...
love is just a heartbeat away

NeXt™

**There's the life you planned.
And there's what comes next.**

⟡ HARLEQUIN®
Presents
Seduction and Passion Guaranteed!

⟡ HARLEQUIN®
Super Romance®

Exciting, Emotional, Unexpected

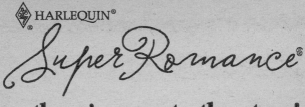
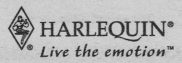